FLAMES

Paul R. Cooper

ISBN 978-0-9896014-1-2

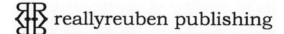 reallyreuben publishing

58 Grandview Avenue
Kingston, NY 12401

Dedicated to the memory of

my brother

Robert L. Cooper

1931-2012

whose unpublished history

New York in Flames

was the source and inspiration

for much of this work.

Acknowledgements

I want to thank my sister-in-law, Alice P. Cooper, who gave me permission to consult the manuscript of her late husband.

Barbara Elsborg, of the UK, gave me the benefit of her usual penetrating criticism and generous encouragement.

My old friend, John Goldman, made some extremely helpful suggestions, which I hope I've put to good use, here.

And I've benefitted not only from my wife Carol's tireless proof reading, but also from her excellent suggestions and unflagging support.

Naturally, any errors or other infelicities are mine alone.

Flames

Forward

The Great Fire of 1835 incinerated a large part of New York City. 674 buildings were destroyed and the look of Manhattan was changed forever. Yet today, this disaster has been largely forgotten. But those who do think of it may see in the glare of that monstrous blaze the dual nature of the city on which it fed: animal appetite on the one hand, and high aspiration on the other. To give a sense of that duality is one of the purposes of this tale, which is peopled with characters both imagined and historical.

Flames

One

A lucky man

"Hold out your hand, young man, so I can count into it a little present for your newborn son—Christopher is his name, I think?"

Joe Simon held out his hand, and his eyes widened as Nehemias Cone put three small gold pieces into it. "Oh, Mr. Cone," he exclaimed, "I don't know how to thank you!"

"No need to thank me—just deliver my shipment as soon as they get it out of the hold of that ship over there," said Cone, indicating the brig *Cassiopeia,* just arrived from London, and docked alongside of dozens of other tall-masted ships in New York's South Street wharves. The year was 1834, and the assembly of all those masts, restless in the quickening wind, gave the sense that the ships knew they had paused here only temporarily, and were eager to be off again.

"I know it's in there, Mr. Cone, I saw the manifest," said Joe, who felt that of all Cone's gifts to him, his helping him learn to read may have been the most valuable. "Don't worry, sir, as soon as they hoist it up, I'll be there to cart it to you. You can be sure of it."

"That I am, lad—you've been as good as gold. Buying you that cart was one of the best investments I ever made."

"Well, I can't thank you enough for it."

"If you insist on thanking me, you can thank me by staying well."

"Sir?"

"I know you like to sing when you work—and that's a good thing. But not on the docks, not around here. There are a lot of longshoremen looking for an excuse to beat up a black man—especially one who looks like he's enjoying himself. I want to see you well. Do you follow me?"

"Oh I do, sir. And I want to see myself well even more than you do! I'll take care."

"Excellent. And now, be off with you; get that cart over to your customer, and deliver his goods. With any luck, by the time you're back here, my shipment will have been brought up, and you can start delivering to me."

"Right away, sir" said Joe, who tipped his brown cap, and walked off, pushing his cart as briskly as if its two hundred fifty pound load were only half its weight. He was a lucky man, he thought, for he had a steady job, and his family, unlike so many of his friends, wasn't starving. He thanked God for Nehemias Cone, and for the family that Cone had helped him to support. Thanks to Cone's latest gift, he'd be sure to finish the day with enough cash to bring home some extra food—maybe even a hunk of smoked ham. How his wife and daughter would love that! Even little Christopher, still nursing, would have a special sense of well being.

What a beautiful day! It was early autumn. The tall ships were so crowded in their East River berths that their assembled masts made Joe think of a stand of watching trees, each bearing witness to the comings and goings on South Street. Were they looking at him? Without slowing his step, he glanced upward to one of the tallest and said, under his breath, "you're watching a lucky man." In the freshening breeze, the pennants on the masts began to snap and crack—in concert, it seemed to him, with the rumble of his cart's wheels on the cobblestones. He found the effect so musical that he began to whistle.

"Hey, nigger! What you whistling for? Why you so happy?"

Joe didn't look to see where the taunt is coming from, but quickened his step. Such gibes were commonplace on the docks. The important thing was to ignore them.

"Hey, nigger! Ain't you gonna stop when I'm talking to you?"

Joe sped up a little more, realizing that there was only so much he *could* speed up without breaking into a run—which was sure to bring out the other white dock workers, who relished any excuse to attack a black man. A run was sure to bring out the dogs.

"Hey you nigger—I'm talking to you! It ain't enough for you blacks to take away our work, you gonna make us run after you?!"

His tormentor grabbed his arm. "Hey, you goddam slave, I'm talking to you!"

Joe said, "I'm not a slave. I'm a free man—my name's Joe Simon. I got a wife and family. They're waiting for me. Let me go." He shook off the hand, but the white man grabbed his arm again.

"Say let me go *please master,* you black piece of shit."

"You're not my master, I'm a free man—let go!" said Joe, striking the white man to get free of him, then breaking into a run, leaving his cart behind.

"Hey boys!" called the white man, "that black bastard hit me! Get him!"

And other longshoremen, like so many white dogs, emerged as if from nowhere, baying and baring their teeth. A rock stunned Joe on the temple; still he staggered on. But it was useless. If the tall ship masts cared enough to look down, they would have seen the white mob, like beasts, bringing Joe to his knees, drawing his blood, and then—more bestial than beasts—butchering him.

That bloody work done, the longshoremen scuttled away, leaving Simon's body sprawled on South Street. Not long after, Nehemias Cone, having heard the outcries, ran towards the group of on-lookers that were surrounding the corpse. Breaking through them, he saw what was left of Simon. "Oh no," he whispered. "I told him, I told him!" He knelt by the body, then lifted his weeping eyes to heaven, his lips forming the soundless word, *"why?"*

Not too far away, but out of earshot of Joe's final scream, a closed carriage, drawn by two horses, was making its way down Nassau Street. Inside were two women—one, the seventeen-year-old Emily Bender, the other Beatrice, her nanny, a middle-aged black woman. Emily was studying a drawing she held in her lap. "Do you think Daddy will like my new drawing?" she asked Beatrice.

"No question about it, honey chile," Beatrice said. "It's good enough for him to like it even if you *weren't* his daughter."

"But is it so good that he won't mind my interrupting him at work?"

"It's good enough even for that, Emily. But don't worry about interrupting—he'll love the surprise. And he'll tell one of the clerks to get it framed and hung, right away. And all the clerks will compliment you on it. It will make a big impression, don't you think? "

But Emily, looking out the window, had turned pale, for the carriage was going by the skeletal remains of some buildings burnt out by a recent fire. They stood like so many blackened cadavers—sightless, and uneasily propped up. "It's horrible," Emily whispered. Tears had sprung to her eyes, and she was trembling.

"Oh Lord," said Beatrice, "I *told* the coachman not to go by any fire ruins, but he's new. I'll have to tell your father."

"Please don't," Emily said, "I don't want to get the new man into trouble."

"All right, honey chile, I won't for your sake. Still, that young man needs a talking-to, and I'll do it myself. But if it happens again, I'll have to report him. In the meantime, shall I draw the curtains, darlin'?"

"What would be the point?" Emily said. "We'd still be able to smell it."

"You got that right, honey. We can close our eyes to the horror, but we can't shut out the stink."

"What a beautiful picture," exclaimed Thaddeus Bender, Emily's father, having risen from his desk at his office. "Your poor mother would have been proud—you have her talent, Emily."

"Thank you, Daddy."

Thaddeus turned to Beatrice. "There was a fire northward, not far from here. Did the new driver manage to avoid it?"

"Everything is fine," Mr. Bender.

"Glad to hear it," said Thaddeus. "He's a sensible lad; he'll do well." Thaddeus turned back to his daughter. "But isn't this close to the time you're due to meet your friends at the ice cream parlor?"

"I'd rather stay with you, but I suppose you're right, Daddy—we'd better get going."

"Have a good time, Emily," Thaddeus said, "and stay as long as you want. I'll probably get home before you, so when you get back from the outing, you can tell me all about it."

Thaddeus turned to Beatrice. "You'll stay with Emily the whole time, won't you?"

"Of course I will."

"They won't let you into the parlor, you know."

"I'll wait outside like I always do."

"I know you will, Beatrice; I can rely on you."

And so it was that in another neighborhood, about sixteen blocks north, Emily was one of a covey of fashionable seventeen-year-old females, enjoying a Saturday holiday from Mrs. Okill's finishing school, gliding smoothly into the New York Public Gardens, where they could order ice cream. Carefully instructed by Mrs. Okill, the girls tried to give the illusion of floating. Though they were several blocks from the school, in their minds they still could hear Mrs. Okill's customary morning counsel: "Dear children: pretend there's a string attached to your chest, and that string is pulling you up...*up!* You should feel as if you're floating one and one half inches above the ground. One and one half inches—that's all you need, children. Any higher than that strains credulity."

The proprietor, who had seen their approach, was standing in the entranceway, welcoming them by name, and ushering them in. After all had disappeared inside the premises, he approached an imposing, respectably dressed black woman, who had been following the group at a respectful distance. "Beatrice," he told her, "you can wait outside if you like, but a little farther away from the entrance, if you don't mind. We don't want to give our patrons the wrong idea." Beatrice nodded impassively, and took a few steps away from the premises.

Inside, the young ladies were tittering over their dishes of ice cream, and making much of one of their number, Sarah Cunningham, who had just announced her engagement to Edward Bass.

"Well, it's not an *official* engagement, yet," Sarah purred, "for Father hasn't yet given his consent."

"Has Edward asked him yet?" asked a classmate.

"We're waiting for that," Sarah said. "In a month or so, when a big contract comes through, Edward will feel financially secure enough to ask him. Of course, he's more than secure enough for me *right now,* but Edward wants to do everything the right way."

"Of course, of course," cooed another of their number, "Edward's very much the proper gentleman. But how did he propose?"

"Well, he told me he loved me..."

"Had he said so before?"

"Not in so many words, although I knew he loved me very much. But he felt that an avowal of love should be accompanied by a proposal of marriage—and he wasn't quite ready for that yet."

"Again, the proper gentleman," said another, "doing that the right way, too."

"Oh!" cried Sarah, "he does *everything* the right way."

"Kissing included?"

Sarah blushed. "Margaret, my dear, it was his kisses I was thinking of."

A chorus of laughter ensued, causing more blushes from Sarah, which in turn caused even more laughter from her friends.

When the hilarity died down, Margaret said, "I do declare that—what with Viola's engagement a fortnight ago, and Jessica's a month prior—we'll all be engaged before this coming June—all that is, except Emily Bender here, who drags that black chaperone around with her wherever she goes. To marry Miss Bender, a man might feel he was robbing the cradle!" By this time, sure of her audience, Margaret got up and carried on: "Big, black Beatrice," she declaimed, comically drawing herself up to her full four-foot seven inches to parody Beatrice's statuesque carriage, "can you imagine the prospect of a wedding night with *her* in the bedroom acting as chaperone even there?!" Howls of laughter greeted this latest sally.

"Oh Margaret, please," said Sarah, "that's mean; it's cruel. Emily is obeying her father. Surely you should not reproach her for that."

"Ah, but even more surely," said Margaret, "she could ask her father to stop insisting that Negress go with her everywhere—she could say it embarrasses her."

Emily had been listening to all this with a demure smile frozen on her face. "But it does *not* embarrass me, Margaret" she said, wishing herself anywhere else, and remembering Beatrice's saying, "if your poor mother were alive, she'd tell you that sometimes it's safest to speak the simple truth."

So, making sure that her smile was still pasted on her face, Emily said, "Beatrice is my good friend; I feel comfortable with her. I feel safe. Besides, Papa has gone to great lengths to provide for me, and to go against him in this would be ungrateful to say the least—perhaps even uncivil."

At this all the other young ladies erupted in more hilarity—all, that is, except Sarah, who reached out sympathetically to touch Emily, whose smile by now had vanished.

A young married couple, on their way out, stared curiously at the cause of all the laughter, and Emily, resisting the impulse to hide her face in her hands, stared red faced right back at them, saying as boldly as she could manage, "my friends appear to find me amusing. You're welcome to join in their laughter, if it pleases you."

The young couple shrugged and proceeded out into the street, where they encountered Beatrice. The young woman offered her a few coins, but Beatrice demurred: "Thank you very much, ma'am, but I don't need the money. Why don't you save it for someone who does?"

As soon as the couple had moved well beyond Beatrice, the woman erupted: "Did you hear that...that...*nigger*...did you hear her refusing our charity?"

"Didn't you recognize her?" said her husband. "She's the servant of our new neighbor—Bender. I believe he's a banker. Doubtless he treats her so well she doesn't need it."

"It'll be a cold day in Hell before I offer her anything else!"

"Calm down," he said, "and don't worry about it. That should be the worst thing that happens to you all week."

"If we lived in Bloomingdale," she retorted, "we wouldn't have to worry about having neighbors like that."

Presumably without such worries, in Bloomingdale itself (in the Northwest corner of the island), a family had gathered for a late lunch within an elegant mansion. There was a modest nosegay of flowers on the table, but two black servants entered—one to remove it, and the second to replace it with a far more impressive floral arrangement. "I hope these flowers please you better, Ma'am," the second servant said.

"I like it very much better," said Martha Livingston, the great lady at the head of the table. "On the rare occasion of Benjamin's gracing us with his presence, a bouquet like this is the least we can do to acknowledge the honor my son is doing us." She gave an arch look in Benjamin's direction, where he was seated at the other end of the table.

"Such a long speech, Mother," said Benjamin. "I wonder if it won't make you too tired to eat anything."

"That will be enough impertinence from you, young man!" she snapped. Then, softening her tone, she told the second servant, "thank you very much, Susie; you did well."

Susie beamed, curtsied, and disappeared.

"What a sweet person," Benjamin said.

"Indeed, she is," said his mother, "as were her parents before her, and their parents before them, and so forth, for more than a hundred years. For as long as I've heard tell, there hasn't been a sour apple in the lot."

"We've been lucky to have them."

"Oh yes, to be sure. But *they've* been lucky to have *us.* We treat them right, and they, in return, are loyal and know their place. We've had good luck with our blacks—they're much better than the Irish, who are apt to get married without any warning."

Benjamin raised an eyebrow. "Don't the negroes want to get married, too?"

"Of course they do," replied his mother, "but they do so at *our* convenience, not at theirs. Oh no. When it comes to servants, give me *a real black every time.*"

Katherine Greene, an eighteen-year-old sitting at table to Benjamin's right, looked uncomfortable. "All this doesn't sound right to me," she said.

"Nor to me," said Benjamin. "Let's change the subject."

"Gladly," said Martha. "What I'd really rather talk about is what you've been up to—as if I couldn't guess."

"You'd guess correctly, Mother."

"Fooling around, then, doubtless?"

"Fooling? What a dismissive word! I've been in Albany—"

"That far away?" his mother interrupted.

"You often have to go *at least* that far to find a worthwhile opportunity, mother," said Benjamin, "and my opportunity is to assist Colonel Stevens in strengthening fortifications. My spare time I devote to a young lady who is just wonderful...wonderful in every way. The fact that she's my Colonel's daughter doesn't hurt either."

"What doesn't it hurt?" asked his mother.

"My quest for glory—or something like it. Perhaps you've heard the saying: 'Victory in the courts of Venus is linked to glory on the battlefields of Mars'? That proverb's well known."

"Not to me it isn't. I've never heard such tripe."

"In plain language, then: If I win the heart of the Colonel's daughter, I might win a greater commission, and a chance to distinguish myself as a leader in battle."

"Oh, my God!" exclaimed Katherine, "wouldn't it be safer to gain glory at home?"

"My sweet Katherine," Benjamin said, "the more safety, the less chance for glory. That's just the way it is. The surest way to find glory is to leave home. The surest way to find *anything* is to leave home."

"What nonsense!" said his mother. "Forget far away battlefields, Benjamin. Simply face up to the trials of everyday—and be loyal, faithful, and true. In that there's glory enough for any real man."

"Mother, I think not."

"Well, think again! It's time to grow up! Settle down in the place that was meant for you," said Martha Livingston with no little asperity. "If you're looking for opportunity, you'll find plenty of it staring you in the face right here, if you'd only open your eyes. And as for a wonderful young woman, you need look no further than—"

"I beg you, Mrs. Livingston, please leave him alone!" Katherine cried. "Maybe if you didn't prompt him so much, he'd come home more often."

"Katherine!" exclaimed Abigail Livingston, her guardian and the Great Lady's sister-in-law, sitting across from Katherine.

Katherine rose from her seat.

"Did we give you leave to rise, young lady?" Abigail asked.

"Forgive me, everyone; I'm not hungry. And I'm feeling...I need some air. Please excuse me," she said, and left the company.

"You see what you've done, Benjamin?" said the Great Lady.

"What *I've* done? Forgive me Mother, but I too have lost my appetite." And Benjamin rose and turned to go.

"You wait just a moment, Benjamin Livingston," said his mother, "you don't have permission to leave the table."

"Allow me to remind you, Mother," said Benjamin, indicating the military uniform he was wearing, "that I am twenty-six, and a Lieutenant in this state's National Guard. Forgive me, but I think it not so wild an ambition to be free of your apron strings. If it's time for me to grow up, then it's time for *you* to realize I do not need your permission for anything." And with that, Benjamin stalked out.

Abigail Livingston looked at her sister-in-law. "Well, Martha," she said, "there went another luncheon, ruined."

The Great Lady sighed irritably. "What did I do, Abigail? Why is it always my fault?"

"I don't know," said Abigail, "but I think I'd better have a word with Katherine." And she left to look for her ward.

She found her in Martha's English garden. She had paused on the graveled path surrounding a small pond, overlooking which stood the "Muses' Temple"—a rotunda with a circular colonnade. This was the place reserved by the landscape architect for quiet reflection, and it was here that Abigail angrily confronted her ward. "Benjamin Livingston is a playboy who needs to grow up," she said. "He's not worth worrying about. If only you'd open your eyes, you'd see you could do a lot better. You're beautiful and rich, and there are—"

"Aunt Abigail, I happen to own a mirror," Katherine interrupted, "and I can see that I'm not beautiful. Maybe decent looking, perhaps, but **certainly *not* beautiful**. False flattery from you serves nobody."

"It is not flattery, and it is not false. Anybody paying attention to you can see how lovely a woman you are. And if they can't, you don't want them, anyway. But there are plenty of men—*grownups*—who'd be glad to pay attention, if only you'd give them a chance! They don't come around anymore because you've made it plain you're not interested."

Katherine suppressed her irritation. "I know you mean well, Aunt Abigail, but there's no use telling me that Benjamin's not worth worrying about. Every time he leaves on militia business, I do worry that I may never see him again. Certainly he has some growing up to do, but he's well worth waiting for."

"You can do better."

"I want no better. As far as I'm concerned, there *is* no better. Please, Aunt Abigail, I hope you won't bother me about it further." Abigail stamped her foot, turned, and thumped back into the house. After she disappeared, Katherine slowly ascended the rise past the Muses' Temple and toward the promontory, from whose eminence she would be able to see Livingston's great estate swooping down to the river bank.

Nehemias Cone opened the door to Cone's Custom Clothing, his specialty shop at the corner of Pine and Williams Streets, and took a weary step inside. "Father!" cried Rachel, his daughter, "you look terrible! What happened?"

"Wait," he said, "let me close the door behind me, lest the neighbors hear of this any sooner than they have to." He closed the door behind him and sank onto one of the wooden chairs provided for customers or their spouses.

By this time, Rachel had come from behind the counter. "Are you all right, Father?" she said, rushing to him. "Can I bring you anything?"

"No, no, my dear, just sit next to me." Rachel did so, then reached over to cover Nehemias' hand with her own, which her father, in turn, covered with his other hand. "My child," he said, "Joe Simon is dead..."

"Oh no!"

"Killed in a race riot."

"Oh my God! How did it happen?"

"I'm not sure; it was a few minutes after he left me on South Street. But I know the white longshoremen have been looking for an excuse for something like this, and Joe could have given them that excuse by whistling or singing—I warned him against it."

"Poor Joe! Poor Mrs. Simon, and her poor children!"

"I know."

"And poor *you*, father. Joe was like a son to you."

"I can't deny it; everyone knows it. With the result that the white carters aren't eager to work for me, and the black ones are afraid to. But I found a white carter with less work than he needs, and bribed him with a bonus. We'll see how that works out."

There was a brief silence.

"Poor Joe," Nehemias said.

"Yes—and poor *us,*" Rachel said.

"You're thinking that something like this could happen to us, aren't you?"

"Yes," she said, "but we have to remember that we have advantages that weren't available to Joe."

"We have many. But which in particular are you thinking of?"

"Well, it's easier for us to blend in, because our skins are white. All we have to do is keep from standing out, and we have a much better chance, around here."

"You're right, my dear. Although there may come a time when we will have no choice but to stand out."

"Why would we need to stand out?" Rachel asked.

"When you stand up for what you believe, it's hard *not* to stand out. Let's hope that the need for that doesn't happen any time soon."

"Amen. And in the meantime, shall we think about how we can help the widow Simon?"

"What do you suggest?"

"Didn't you say that Mrs. Simon can sew?"

"Yes, Joe told me that."

"Well, every so often I have more sewing to do than I can handle, and now, what with Mr. Bender's large order for shirts, I'll be buried in needlework! But if we hand off some of the other sewing to Mrs. Simon, I could satisfy Mr. Bender's order more quickly."

"Which would be a very good thing."

"Considering who he is?"

"Exactly. If we please him promptly, many more orders may come from other rich bankers. Rachel, this is very good thinking—no matter how you look at it."

Rachel cast her eyes down, demurely. "Thank you, Father." But inwardly, she thought, it's *a nice gesture, but I fear we won't have enough work to make a meaningful difference for Mrs. Simon.*

Elsewhere on Manhattan Island, Emily and Beatrice, walking homeward from the outing at the New York Public Gardens, were deep in discussion. "Robbing the cradle," said Emily, "that's what Margaret was saying: anyone marrying me would feel like a cradle robber."

"Why would she say a thing like that?" Beatrice asked.

"Well—don't be upset, Beatrice—but it was because of your chaperoning me all the time, making me seem...well...young for my age."

'I see."

"*Am* I young for my age? You can tell me the truth, Beatrice: I'm seventeen years old. Do I act it?"

They proceeded a dozen steps without an answer from the older woman, so Emily asked again: "Do I act like I'm seventeen years old, Beatrice, or do I act young for my age? You can tell me."

"Well," said Beatrice, "everyone is different. Some folks act prematurely old, while others never seem to grow up."

"You haven't answered me. Is this your way of telling me that I act immature?"

"Emily, not everyone has a father like yours—who can't stand to see his daughter grow up. He still sees you as his little girl, and, maybe to please him, you act that way."

"And that behavior has become a habit of mine—is that what you're saying?"

"Well, if it *has* become a habit, you're starting to outgrow it."

"Really? How do you know?"

"Because of all these questions you're asking, honey chile!"

They walked on together for some moments before Emily said: "Beatrice, dear, if I were to ask you to stop calling me "honey chile," would you be upset?"

"Of course I would, darlin', because you'll always be my honey chile. But if you wanted it, I'd stop calling you that—I'd have to. Has it come to that?"

"No it has not," said Emily, "nor will it ever. I love hearing you call me honey chile. I would feel so empty if you stopped."

By this time, Emily and Beatrice had arrived at the row house which was their fourth street home, a four-story brick structure, whose entrance sported the neoclassical columns common in that expensive neighborhood. In the second story, Thaddeus Bender sat reading a newspaper in the small office he used at home. Hearing a quiet tap on the door he called, "come in, Emily." Emily opened the door and poked her head in. "Sit down, my dear," said her father, gesturing toward a chair.

But Emily said, "Am I too old to sit on your lap, Daddy?"

"Of course not. You come sit down right here," he said, patting his lap. She did, and he embraced her.

"I'm not too heavy for you, am I?"

"Of course not. You're still my little girl—light as a feather."

She sighed happily, and nestled in, running her fingers through his dense, short cropped, black beard.

He bestowed on her a paternal kiss, and said, "what's troubling you, little one? Is it something that happened in the ice cream parlor?"

"Oh, nothing happened in particular."

"Come on—I know you better than that. When you're perfectly at ease you're content to sit in your grown-up chair over there. But your sitting in my lap tells me you need some special attention."

"No Daddy! It means I love you."

"I know it, baby, and I love you too. But I also know there's something troubling you—am I right?"

"Well, there *is* something…"

"I thought so. Out with it."

"Daddy, is it true that you lend money to Southern plantation owners, and they repay you with cotton?"

Flames

Thaddeus squirmed a little under her, and adjusted her weight on him.

"I *am* too heavy on you!" she cried. "I'll get off."

"No, no, you're fine; it's just me."

"You tell me when I'm too heavy, and I'll get off—all right?"

"Emily: whether or not I have commerce with Southern plantation owners—is it so important to you?"

"It's *very* important, Daddy. I'd hate to think of you making money off the suffering of slaves. But you wouldn't do that, would you?"

Thaddeus reached for an answer and then slowly replied, "Not willingly, Emily." On his face he arranged a reassuring smile. "Before you were born, I used to do some of that sort of thing, and some people think I still do. But now, not really. Now, I mainly do Northern business loans and home mortgages."

"I'm so glad!"

"It means that much to you?"

"I feel bad when the girls say you're involved with slave owners. Because that would make you a partner in all their crimes, and I know you'd never go along with that."

"It sounds like you have an abolitionist for a teacher."

"Miss Turin—yes. She's very strong on the subject—or was. They fired her last week."

"I daresay."

"What do you mean, you daresay? She's a very good teacher—made a big impression on us."

"Apparently! But good as she may be, your teacher didn't show good judgment. New York is not a good city to preach the abolition of slavery."

"Why not?"

"When you grow up you'll understand why."

"Daddy, I'm grown up, now!"

She tried to get off his lap, but he restrained her, saying "I mean, *more* grown up. You still have a little growing to do. Which is why I'm glad you're still going to Mrs. Okill's school."

"Well *I'm* not," said Emily, pouting. "That place is so...superficial. They spend so much time on when to present your visiting card, and what to write on it, and what corner to fold! We're all taught a little bit about a lot of things, so we can have pleasant conversations with our husbands—as if getting married is the be all and end all of a woman's life."

"Well, isn't it?"

"Daddy! Marriage is important, but it's not the *only* thing. Nowadays there's a lot more a woman can do. Let me up!" With effort, she forced him to release her, and she rose. "Nowadays," she said, warming to her theme, "women can be involved in reforms, if they want to—not only in the abolition of slavery, but also in temperance, education, and the enfranchisement of women."

"Ho! No wonder Miss Turin got fired."

"**Daddy**! *I'd* like to be involved in some of these reforms."

"I keep saying the wrong things, don't I?"

"No, Daddy—not exactly..."

"Emily, darling, let me tell you something: it's all very well to have opinions of your own. You poor mother had plenty, and I loved her *because* of them, since one of them was...that I was worth loving."

"Well, of course you are, Daddy!"

"Your mother's parents didn't think so. I was born poor, and your mother's folks couldn't see beyond that. But your mother could, and I loved her for it. As for her other opinions, she was a bit of a rebel—like you—but she had the good sense to keep her rebellious notions to herself."

"What good is it to have rebellious notions if you have to keep them all to yourself?"

"Everyone has secrets, Emily; it's the way of the world. And when you are out of the house, you must keep yours. But *in* your home, surrounded by people you trust, then you can be more open. And when you meet your soul mate, Emily, you must confide to him *everything,* and he will likewise confide in you. In fact, every family member should be able to trust you whenever you say anything important."

"Like when you tell me you no longer have any business with slave owners, Daddy, right?"

"Still on that?" Thaddeus rose and enfolded his daughter in his arms. "Yes, darling," he said, "You're all I have. I never want to speak an untruth to you." And then he added, quietly, "if I can help it."

"I love you, Daddy."

He patted her reassuringly, but on his face was a troubled expression as he gazed out the Tudor-styled window, whose warped glass gave a crazed aspect to the city.

Flames

Two
Interest in fire engines

Above the wide, double-doored entranceway was a wooden board whose hand-painted scrawl, "Engine Co. No. 5," suggested its painter was no professional sign maker. However, *inside* the premises, the cleanliness and order gave every indication that its users—volunteer firemen all—regarded their business with high professional seriousness. The solid brass water nozzle was polished to a high gloss, the leather hoses were draped carefully on drying racks, the leather buckets neatly stacked, the axe handles lovingly oiled, their heads cleaned and sharpened to such a well honed edge that the firemen boasted that they had shaved with them. On the walls were several leather presentation shields, each hand painted to express the gratitude of the recipients of their services. Each shield was important to them, but the one most prized was inscribed with the admiration of another fire company.

At present all the firemen were busy cleaning and polishing their prized engine—all, that is, except their young leader, Sean Dougherty, who was polishing his speaking trumpet. While they worked, one of them said, "Sean, lad, tell us again how you carried the banker's daughter to safety last year. And sure, she called you her hero."

"Her hero, is it?" Sean replied. "Nonsense, Timmy! All I did was steady her a little—she was really frightened—then I took her hand and led her down the stairs."

"The *burning* stairs," Timmy said to the others, "he forgets that. And her *Da* calls him a hero. Pulls out his wallet, he does, and he's all ready to be paying him...and the damn fool says, *I'm a volunteer, and do this for love and duty, and I won't be accepting tips from the people I help*...thus givin' the rest of us firemen a bad name. When I heard that, me heart skipped a beat!"

He and the other firemen laughed uproariously. Then he turned back to Sean.

"But now, tell us lad, what did she say to you after you got her outside? And her face was real close to yours and she was whispering something warm 'n lovely to you..."

Sean looked up from polishing the speaking trumpet, but he wasn't seeing anything in the firehouse. *She was so beautiful,* he thought, *like that alabaster cameo Ma brought from Ireland, but with a smudge of soot on it from the fire...ah, what would it have been like to kiss that soot away—especially when she whispered, "are all firemen like you?"*

But his reverie was snapped by the insistence of the other firemen: *"WHAT DID SHE SAY?!"*

"Mother of God!" Sean shouted, "how am I supposed to remember? It's been a year!"

"Only a year is it? You may not remember her, but I'll bet your suspenders she sure remembers *you*—the strong, good lookin' hero of romance that you are!"

"Stop with the romance nonsense. And what is this betting my suspenders? If I accept the bet, what happens if she *does* remember me?"

"You give over your suspenders, me lad, and find another way to hold yer pants up—that is, if you still *want* to hold them up!"

"Timmy, it's *yourself* who is the damn fool. I reckon we got other things to think about besides women."

Flames

"You mean next week's race? We couldn't be better prepared," said Timmy. The engine will gleam like the beauty it is."

"Which won't mean a damn if it's too slow. I think we should get some grease and repack the axles—to give ourselves every advantage."

"Isn't it yerself you want to be giving every advantage—if your young lovely shows up in the crowd?"

"Will you give it a rest?" cried Sean. "She's *not* my young lovely, and if she shows up in the crowd, I might not even recognize her, it's been so long. What I care about right now is getting this speaking trumpet clean."

"Come on, Sean," said someone helpfully, "it's already gleaming so bright it hurts our eyes to look at it."

"Well, it's not bright enough for me," growled the young firefighter, who redoubled his efforts on the device while the smothered laughter among his comrades told him he was fooling no one.

"A firemen's race!" cried Emily to Beatrice. "Can we go?" It was late afternoon, and they were in their home on 4th Street.

Beatrice gave her a probing look. "I'd have thought you'd steer clear of anything reminding you of fire—since you were so badly frightened by the fire last year at our place. You had nightmares about it."

"I still do. But I want to meet the man who saved me— *he* wasn't afraid of the fire. I'll never forget how calm he was. As soon as he touched my hand, I felt safe."

"He certainly was a good lookin' man. I saw him."

Emily sniffed. "His looks are beside the point. It's his courage I want to get closer to."

"I expect you can't get closer to his courage without getting close to the man himself."

"Oh, *you*—always with the most earthy slant on things!"

"Nothing wrong with the earth, child—it's what we walk on."

"Are we going to the race or aren't we?"

"There are a lot of firemen in the city. What if your fireman doesn't show up?"

"I'll be disappointed. Of course I will! But it's worth a try, isn't it?"

"Of course it is, darlin', if it means that much to you. We'll go."

The following Sunday, Beatrice and Emily were in the crowd, which was eager for the excitement to begin. For Emily, however, the excitement already *had* begun, because she had spotted her savior among the racers. There was no mistaking his red-headed countenance—she had memorized it. Her eyes were so riveted on him that in her sight everything surrounding him seemed to fade away, as if she were inflicting on herself some form of tunnel vision. Emily quite forgot that she had dressed in her nicest, narrow-waisted print dress, with its broad shoulders, puffed sleeves, and embroidered neckline; she was conscious only of her fireman, who, like all his fellows, had stripped down to the waist, his manly physique—like theirs—becoming the object of much covert feminine admiration.

Flames

A route circling a few blocks had been cleared for the race. The starter's pistol fired, and the machos began hauling their identical 3000-pound fire engines through the streets. The crowd cheered, and so did Emily, waving her handkerchief madly. But once the firemen disappeared around a bend, a sourpuss in the crowd—a woman in late middle-age—complained to Emily that the race was a scandal. What would happen if a real fire was reported? And even if the firemen heard the fire bell, would they have left enough strength to tow their engines to the fire, let alone fight it? So what was the purpose of this useless exercise? To show off their manly chests to the shameless females in the crowd—that's what!

Beatrice approached her. "If the masculine display offends you madam, you can always walk away from it."

The sourpuss stared at Beatrice. "How dare you...?" She then looked at Emily: "Did you hear what she...?"

"Oh yes," said Emily, smiling blandly. "She said what I think, too."

The sourpuss was undaunted. "Well! This whole thing is stupid. In London, fire engines get to fires as much as 30 minutes earlier than ours do, because they're pulled by horses—not by men eager to show how manly they are. Even you must be able to see how much more sensible that is. How much more forward looking."

Emily looked at her. "You've been to London?"

"Of course. Hasn't everyone?"

After an embarrassed silence, the sourpuss said triumphantly, "Apparently not."

A distant cheer was heard.

"What's that cheer?" Emily asked.

"The firemen have turned the corner," said Beatrice; "and now they're returning."

"I hope my fireman's company is in the lead," said Emily.

"*Your* fireman?" the sourpuss said. "You have your own personal fireman?"

"Only...in a manner of speaking. A fireman saved my life a year ago, and he's racing today, so naturally I want his company to win."

"He saved your life? That must have been exciting."

"It *was* exciting," said Emily, but not nearly as exciting as what happened *afterwards*."

"Oh really! And what happened afterwards, pray tell?"

But the crowd noises were swelling now, and a fire crew was seen in the distance.

"I see them! I see them!" cried Emily, "at least I *think* it's they; I can't tell! I can't tell yet!"

The sourpuss was not giving up. She tapped Emily on the shoulder and said, "all right, little miss, you have me riveted in suspense—what happened after your fireman saved your life? Tell me—tell me what happened! Tell me, you impertinent little thing!"

Emily turned her back on the race as she whirled around to face the sourpuss. "What happened was that I got to talk to him."

"That's it? You got to talk to him? What did you say to him? ***What did you say to him?***"

"Oh...just five words."

"Five words? He's just saved your life and all you can think of to say is five words? What were they?"

Flames

But by this time, Emily had turned back to the race and had seen that her favorite and his company were in the lead. The sourpuss couldn't get through to her; nobody could because her favorite was winning; he had won! Emily was ecstatic.

So apparently, were Sean's crew, which had lifted to their shoulders Sean Dougherty, their leader and hero.

"Beatrice," said Emily, "go over there; please go to him, Beatrice, tell him I want to talk to him."

"Go and tell him yourself."

"I can't! I won't know what to say! Please help me, Beatrice. He'll go away, soon."

"Say this to him," said Beatrice, who whispered something in Emily's ear.

"I'm to go over there and tell him *that?*"

"Think of it as a test," Beatrice said.

"A test? For whom?"

Beatrice was smiling. "Shouldn't you hurry while he's still here?" she said.

"You have to come with me."

"Oh, all right," said Beatrice, who allowed herself to be dragged closer to the street.

"Mr. Fireman! Mr. Fireman!"

When Sean saw Emily running toward him, he asked his comrades to set him down.

And now Emily was close enough to touch him. Her heart was pounding and she was as breathless as if it were she who had just finished the race. "Mr. Fireman...you may not remember me...but a year ago you saved my life."

"I remember."

29

"You do? I would have thought you saved so many lives…"

"Not that many. But even if I saved a thousand, Miss, I could never forget you."

"Oh!"

"And now you want to be thanking me?"

"Well, what I wanted to say…is that every Sunday I worship at the Methodist Church nearby and I'd love…uh…to see you there, too."

"You're telling me that you want me to come to the Methodist Church this coming Sunday?"

"Well, yes, I just thought…"

Sean smiled broadly. "Miss, are you serious? I'm Roman Catholic!"

"Sorry…I just thought…" *This isn't going very well.*

"Surely you're not serious!"

Does he think I'm joking?

But then Beatrice, summoning all her considerable dignity, said "Mr. Fireman: my lady *is* serious. She couldn't be more so."

O my God, she's forward…and so am I!

Sean looked at Beatrice. "I'll be there," he told her. He looked at Emily, and said to her, smiling, "I wouldn't miss it."

Emily caught her breath. *It's too late, now. But who cares—I wouldn't miss it, either!*

"What do you mean, you think you've fallen in love with a fireman?" The voice belonged to Thaddeus Bender, at his home, several hours after the race.

"It just happened today, Daddy, and you've told me that when I'm in the house I can be honest with my feelings."

Flames

Thaddeus softened. "Well...you were quite right to speak of them to me, my dear; I'm glad I know of it. But I hope I don't have to tell you that a relationship with a man of that class would be most unwise. It's not only that he hasn't the money to support you. It's also that, very likely, he hasn't been schooled to control his passions, and that he would bring you nothing but grief."

"Oh, no, Daddy," Emily began, "This man's not like that."

"Are you contradicting me, my dear?" said a smiling Thaddeus, behind whom was Beatrice, shaking her head, then placing a warning finger to her lips.

This warning had the desired result: "Oh no, Father, you are right. I'll be careful NOT to fall in love with him."

"Best not to see him again."

"I understand, Father. You're right," Emily said. But what she thought was: *I gave in so quickly, with scarcely an argument...does Daddy actually* believe *me, or does he merely* pretend *to believe me? He may well be pretending: after all, I'm pretending to agree with* him. *So much for honesty! Each of us is lying, and hoping that the other will pretend not to know it.*

Flames

Three
You're a Greater Fool than I Took You For

Sean Dougherty, bouquet in hand, was approaching one of a row of dilapidated houses in Five Points, a slum in New York. He walked up to a door indistinguishable from the others on the street, put the bouquet behind his back, and knocked on the door. After a moment, the door was opened by a tidy, gray-haired lady. "Hi Ma," he said.

"Sonny! What are you doin', knockin' at my door like a stranger or somethin'? You gave me a fright," she said, waving her gnarled, hickory cane at him; "I thought you were a Watchman or somethin', and I scarcely dared to—"

Sean interrupted her by producing the bouquet. "Uh-oh," she said, "what trouble have you got yourself into this time, that you need pacify me with flowers?"

"No trouble, no trouble, Ma; I just figured you deserved a bouquet once in a while."

"When I believe that, you can sell me a three-headed chicken."

"Can I come in, or are you going to make me stand out in the street holding these flowers like a fool?"

"Give me the flowers and come on in. Wash yer hands, and sit down. And as soon as I get these flowers in water, I'll serve you supper, and you can tell me the truth."

Megan Dougherty seized the bouquet, and, aided by her cane, stumped back into her little two-room house, which, though austere, was as clean and neat on the inside as the street outside was filthy. Soon Sean was sitting on a rough-hewn bench before a table of similar construction, and Megan was putting in front of him a plate heaped full of Colcannon, consisting mainly of mashed potatoes, kale, and butter. To herself she gave only a modest portion. They bowed their heads and she said, "Bless us O Lord and these Thy gifts, which we are about to receive from Thy bounty through Christ our Lord, Amen." For a minute they ate with little conversation; he complimented her on her cooking, and she dismissed his good words as empty flattery.

"Now then, you've got some food in you, so I'm thinking you'll have the stomach to tell me the truth: what are the flowers for?"

"The truth is I love you, Ma…"

"Oh, get on with you."

"And also, it's a very busy season at the warehouse, and Mr. Tappan wants us to stay late for a few days…"

"Aha! So that's it!"

"He'll be serving us supper to keep our strength up" said Sean a little more quickly, as if to forestall his mother's wrath. "It'll be only until we can get the new stock in and sorted, and catch up on all the back orders…"

"And how long will *that* be, pray tell?"

"I'm not sure. Shouldn't be more than a few days, I should think."

"So: it's not bad enough that heathen makes you sleep in a dormitory, he deprives me of my suppers with you!"

"He's not a heathen, Ma."

"He's a *Protestant* and will be damned to Hell for it."

"Arthur Tappan is a godly man."

"A Protestant godly? That's blasphemy if ever I heard it."

Flames

"He starts the workday with prayers—"

"*Protestant* prayers—"

"Prayers are prayers, for Heaven's sake! And the one God above hears *all* prayers, no matter if they're in Latin or English, and He loves everybody, whether or not they acknowledge the Pope."

"Saints preserve us, they've got to you already. Now I know why they're keeping you late, and making you sleep in the dormitory."

"You know no such thing."

"They want to seduce your mind!"

"Oh God, it's nothing like that—no! As I said, we're staying late to catch up on business. And as I've been saying, the dormitory is only for us unmarried men, so we won't get into trouble. Arthur Tappan has our best interests at heart. He's looking out for us."

"Not nearly so well as I would, given half a chance." Megan started gathering up her plates to bring them to the wash basin. Sean began gathering up his, but Megan said, "you've scarcely had one helping, Sonny. Sit. Eat."

"I'm all right Ma, I've had plenty." As he brought his plates to the wash basin, he said, "would you prefer I went back to working at the docks? I couldn't afford then to buy good food for us, let alone bring you flowers. C'mon Ma—what are you afraid of?"

"The truth, Sean boy, is that I'm afraid of what sort of girl you're going to bring home to me."

"Only someone you could love."

"But will she be Catholic?"

"Ma, I hope so."

"What do you mean, you hope so? She had better *be* so!"

"Ma, this is a big city, and I'm doing the best I can. But the only way to guarantee a Catholic girl friend is to move back to Ireland. You want that?"

"If only yer father were home, instead of working in Boston, he'd kick some sense into yer head."

"No doubt he'd try. Look Ma, thanks for supper—it was delicious, and I'm grateful. I gotta get back to the dorm a little early…"

"Why now?"

"Mr. Tappan wants to see how I do with calculating accounts. I need some time to make sense of them."

"You can hardly wait to take your leave of me, right, Seanie?"

"I love it when you call me Seanie. C'mon, Ma, I love you. Give me a kiss."

"Get on with you; you're twenty-one years old. If you don't know I love you by this time, you're a greater fool than I took you for."

Flames

Four
Better a quick death than a slow one

At a large construction site, several hundred striking stone cutters, dressed in work clothes, and carrying banners in addition to their hammers and other heavy tools, were confronting the 27th Regiment of the National Guard, all with arms at the ready. Leading them was a Colonel, who, in a commanding voice, shouted at the crowd, "You are ordered to disperse and go home!"

A stone cutter shouted back, "so, they've called out the troops, have they? What are you going to do—kill us all?"

"You are disturbing the peace and destroying public property. This building is going to be New York University. Go home! My name is Colonel Adam Stevens, and I have orders to shoot to kill if necessary."

A burly man, apparently the leader of the strike, approached saying "I don't care if you're General George Washington! We used to be the ones cutting the stone for this building, but it's now being cut by prison labor up the river in Sing Sing. They work for nothing! And do you know where that leaves us and our families? We're starving to death!"

He extracted a hammer from his tool belt, and with both fists clenched, shook it at the Colonel. "Better a quick death than a slow one," he told him. Then he shouted to his confederates, "go ahead boys, continue the wrecking job, and let these dogs do their worst!"

"So what happened?" asked Katherine. She, Abigail, Martha, and Benjamin were sitting around the Livingstons' dining room table. "Tell us, Benjamin," she asked again, "what happened?"

"We fired over their heads," said Benjamin, "and they scattered, thank God. I didn't want to order my men to shoot to kill."

"That would have been no more than they deserved," said Abigail, pouring some claret into her crystal goblet. "If those Irishmen don't want to starve, let them learn a trade more skilled than stone cutting."

But Katherine shook her head, and looked directly at Benjamin. "Would you have ordered your men to shoot to kill?"

"I'm afraid I'd have had no choice, Kate," Benjamin answered. "If I obey only the orders I agree with, I have no business being in the Service."

"I wish you weren't," said Katherine. "Then, when you went away, I might not have to worry about whether I'd ever see you again."

Benjamin smiled at Katherine. "You're very sweet," he said. "But I became a citizen-soldier because that's what my father was—may God rest his soul. He died a hero..."

"But not in battle," said Martha. "He was killed fighting a fire. My dear Katherine: when the men walk out of the house, we never know whether we're *ever* going to see them again."

Flames

Five

Your name has been a prayer on my lips

"It's all in the hands of God," the Methodist minister intoned. "May He bless you all with a peaceful Sabbath, and a prosperous week." A small bellows organ began playing, the minister headed solemnly to his position outside the church, near the front door, and the congregation began filing out to greet him.

To get to this moment, Emily had made her way through thickets of prayers, and had endured an unusually long sermon. She had forced herself to look nowhere else but at her hymnal, on which she had focused with such force that it was a wonder, she thought, that the holy book had not caught fire. But now, solemnly proceeding down the aisle toward the front door, her eyes devotedly focused on her folded hands, she felt that only one more time must she mentally rehearse the ruse Beatrice had gone over with her repeatedly this past week. *In just minutes*, she thought excitedly, *it will begin.*

Once Thaddeus had exchanged greetings with the minister, Emily glanced at Beatrice, who nodded almost imperceptibly. *Now is the time.* "Oh!" cried Emily, "I've left my bag inside, on the pew. Will you come with me Beatrice, to help me get it?"

"Go ahead, Beatrice," Thaddeus said, "I'll wait here till you both return."

Emily's eyes appealed to Beatrice to perform the next step.

"Mr. Bender," Beatrice said, "you're probably hungry, and I've instructed Cook to have ready for you your favorite hot chocolate and tea biscuits, so there's no need for you to wait. You just go on ahead and enjoy, and we'll meet you at home."

"All right, Beatrice, thanks; I don't mind if I do. I'll see you in a few minutes." And with that, Thaddeus strode away, his silver-handled cane swinging superbly.

It worked, it worked! Emily thought, *God bless you, Beatrice!* Eyes shining, Emily turned to Beatrice and murmured, "I can't thank you enough."

"Don't even try," said Beatrice. "Just go back in there and meet your fireman."

"He's there?"

"Certainly."

"You saw him?"

"Of course."

"I was afraid to look."

"I knew you were, so I made sure. Let's go back in. And when you're inside, don't look for him. Let him find you."

Back in the sanctuary, just as Emily picked up the bag, and held it close, Sean emerged from the shadows. With a sharp intake of breath, Emily sensed his presence, then turned to see him. Her heart was thudding in her chest, and only with a great deal of effort did she manage to get out: "I did so hope we'd meet here."

"And so did I," he replied, "although when I saw your Da, I didn't know how you'd manage it."

"I wasn't sure either—until Beatrice here gave me the idea."

"I'm grateful to you, Miss Beatrice," he said.

Beatrice nodded.

"I wanted to tell you," Emily said, "How much I—how much *Beatrice* and I—admired your run...your *whole fire*

40

company's run, of course...and how much we *both* would love to get a closer look at your fire engine...we both are *very* interested in fire engines, aren't we Beatrice?"

"I suppose so."

"*Of course* we are! Anything that keeps us safer from fire—it's our duty to be interested in it—wouldn't you agree, Beatrice?"

"Yes, miss."

Emily turned her attention back to Sean: "And so, Mr. Fireman, we both were wondering if someday...if you had the time...and it wouldn't be too much trouble...if we both could make a visit there...and you could show the engine to us..."

"This is all right with your Da?"

"He knows I'm always safe so long as Beatrice is with me."

"She goes everywhere with you?"

Now it comes...he'll think he's robbing the cradle! But I better tell him the truth...

"Yes, wherever I go, she comes too...if you don't mind very much. I feel...more comfortable when she's around." *I feel safer, too—but he doesn't have to know that.*

"Well, I would want you...that is, *the whole company* would want you to feel comfortable, Miss Emily."

"You know my name!"

"Ever since I got you out of that burning house last year, I made it my business to learn it, and remember it."

"You have the advantage of me, Mr. Fireman: I don't know *your* name."

"My name is Sean Dougherty. The name is not known to fame, but I'm hoping you'll remember it, for all that."

"Oh, I will. And Beatrice and I would love to visit your fire company. Do you think you could write down its address?"

"I have it already written down. I was hoping you would ask," he said, as he handed her a slip of paper.

As she took it, she blushed. *Oh! He* knew *I'd be forward and ask! Am I very bad? Maybe—but it's too late now!* And mastering her voice to make it sound relaxed and poised, she said, "Thank you Mr. Dougherty. We'll come to you next Sunday at 2:30. I hope you can remember my name for one more week."

"For many months, Miss Emily, your name has been a prayer on my lips. I'm not like to forget it."

"A prayer on my lips...!" Emily mused out loud as Beatrice and she were walking home after their churchly encounter with Sean. "I can't get over that he said that."

"I've heard that the Irish are masters of flattery," Beatrice told her, "so at this stage I wouldn't give it too much thought."

Emily looked a bit deflated. "You mean he was being insincere?"

"At the firehouse next week, we may begin to find out."

"Seven whole days," said Emily. "That's a long time to wait."

"Busy yourself with other things," Beatrice said. "A week will go by before you know it."

At the firehouse, a week later, the firemen eagerly awaited the arrival of Emily and Beatrice. "Well, Sean boyo," cried Patrick, "ain't you the fine figure of romance! Shoes shined, pants pressed—you even took a bath, saints preserve us, and cleaned your nails!"

"I'll have to admit, Patrick, I did prepare somewhat for the occasion. But you're not too shabby yourself, now that I look at you."

"Why single out him?" cried a fellow fireman; "What about *me?*" asked another.

"You're all of you more than presentable," said Sean, "you're even handsome...and yet...that won't be nearly enough."

"What more do you want, me lad?" said Timothy, "should we have put on perfume?"

"Of course not, Timmy. But what I expect more than anything is *courtesy* to the ladies. That's worth ten times all the rest."

"You wouldn't be casting aspersions on my sainted mother, would you, and on the training she gave me?"

"Not in the slightest. I'm sure she *tried* to bring you up right, and to give you good rules to live by. The question is, will you remember 'em?"

"She taught me to scrub my face in the mornin,' and just look," Timothy said, thrusting his face almost into Sean's, "I'm bright and shinin'!"

"And it's a tribute to your sainted mother, that it is, Timmy. And yet—meaning no disrespect to her memory—I have to tell you that *anybody* can scrub his face clean. The question is: can you scrub your *thoughts* clean? That's what I'd like here."

"Listen to him!" cried Timmy, "he wants us to have not only clean faces, but freshly scrubbed thoughts too, wouldn't you know! Well, what *I* want to know is, who elected *him* Pope?"

"I'm no Pope, you idiot, but I *am* the head of this out-fit—and if I get the slightest sense of disrespect from any of you apes, I'll beat the stuffing out of you. You get it?"

But before Timmy could answer, the door knocker was heard. Someone moved to the door, but Sean arrested him with a loud, *"I'LL GET IT!"* He strode to the door, opened it, and was rewarded by the sight of Beatrice and Emily, the latter tremulously smiling. Sean whipped off his cap, whereupon the rest of the crew, taking his cue, whipped off theirs—all, that is, except Timmy, who stood rigidly at attention, his cap on his head. Patrick, standing next to him and seeing this delinquency, whipped off Timmy's cap and slammed it into his stomach.

"Please, ladies, do come in," said Sean. Beatrice and Emily entered, and Sean said: "Miss Emily and Miss Beatrice, allow me to present to you the members of Engine Company No. 5." The firemen all muttered greetings, bowed or waved in their several ways, and Emily bobbed a cute little curtsey. Turning to his comrades, Sean said, "the ladies watched our win a couple of weeks ago..."

"Oh yes, it was wonderful!" Emily said.

"...and they asked could they visit our firehouse, and I said you gentlemen would be glad to show them around."

"Indeed we would, and there's a lot to see!" cried Timmy.

"There's our collection of pry-bars of all different sizes," said Patrick...

"A pry-bar for every job," said another...

"And a fine assortment of fire-axes," one more said.

"But be careful how you touch 'em; they're sharp as razors," put in one of the older men.

"You can l-look at our m-maintenance schedule," said someone normally ill at ease in speaking publicly..."We r-rotate jobs. We all have j-jobs to do—even Sean, here!"

Another said, "Don't forget the tribute shields we won!"

"I hope you won't forget the fire engine," said Emily, "I do want to see that!"

Timmy responded, "we'll save the best for the last. Shall we get started?"

And the men began to take Emily around the firehouse; Beatrice had elected to stand with Sean at a place elevated enough to allow them to oversee the proceedings.

"Thank you for your kindness, Mr. Dougherty," said Beatrice. "It looks like Miss Emily is enjoying herself thoroughly."

"I certainly hope so, Miss Beatrice. I had no idea that firefighting was so appealing to her. Is she really that interested?"

"Her interest in firefighting is genuine enough—so far as it goes."

"What about you, Miss Beatrice? Why are *you* here?"

Beatrice gave Sean a look that would frighten a basilisk, and declared: "To make sure Miss Emily doesn't get burned."

"Heaven forbid."

Beatrice smiled at the young man, and he smiled in return. Then she said, "that is a charming sign outside your firehouse," Mr. Dougherty. Where did you find the painter?"

"Timothy's Aunt painted it. Chief Engineer Gulick thinks we should get another, but I won't do that. It would hurt Timothy's feelings, and besides, we don't need a fancy sign to show how good we are. You see that tribute shield over there? That was presented to us by another fire company no less, in admiration of our work. Now *they* have a professional sign in front of their fire house, but we don't need one. We *know* we're good."

By this time, the firefighters had taken Emily to the fire engine itself, and were explaining to her how the "brakes"—the pumping handles—work. After they demonstrated the pumping action, she said, "may I try it? I'd like to get the feel of it," to which Timmy replied, "you go ahead and get the feel of whatever you like, Miss Emily."

This sparked Sean's anger, and he took a murderous step towards Timmy, only to be restrained by Beatrice. "Let him be," she said, "the poor fool doesn't know any better."

The firemen lowered a brake to a height where Emily could readily seize it. She reached up and tried her best to move it. "Oh!" she cried, "this is hard work—you gentlemen must be very strong."

"We generally have at least six men to a brake," said Patrick, "eight is better—but even then we can go only a few minutes before we have to rest."

"Then the next team takes over," said another.

Emily thanked them for their time and their courtesy, and made her way to where Sean and Beatrice had been watching. "This has been so fascinating, Mr. Dougherty," Emily said, "I can't thank you enough."

"Shall I show you some sites of recent fires, Miss Emily? In their way, they are fascinating, too."

Flames

Beatrice interposed: "I'm not sure that would be a good idea, Mr. Dougherty. Miss Emily might react badly to anything reminding her of—"

But Emily interrupted: "Excuse us, Mr. Dougherty, but Beatrice and I need to confer." She hustled Beatrice into a far corner. "What are you saying?" asked Emily, *sotto voce,* "I want to see it—I really want to see it!"

"But since last year," whispered Beatrice with similar hushed intensity, "you've been making the coachman take a wide detour around all fire ruins—you said you didn't want to be reminded!"

"That was then. But now, I feel I must try to face up to things. I have to! Can we go...*please?*"

Beatrice smiled at her. "Go ahead then, honey chile. You go face up to things."

So Emily and Beatrice returned to Sean. "Mr. Dougherty," Emily said, "we accept your invitation with thanks. It is *very important* for us to look at fire ruins. It is our duty."

When Sean, Emily and Beatrice left, Emily graced the firemen with a very deep curtsey, causing all the firemen to bow, this time deeply, as one man.

"What fun that was," Emily said, once outside. But Sean was clearly upset. "When you worked the brakes," he said, "all the men were thinking...impure thoughts."

"Oh, no," she said. "Surely you imagined it."

"They were like beasts."

"Oh dear. Did I do something wrong?"

"You did nothing wrong, Miss Emily. When an angel like you is in the room, all men become beasts."

Beatrice smiled sardonically. "Including you, Mr. Dougherty?"

"If I had any bestial thoughts, may I go without food for a week!"

"And what good would that do?" inquired Beatrice.

"Starve the beast in me, it would!"

Flames

Six
A matter of policy

Thaddeus Bender, on his way to enjoy a mid-day snack, was strolling through the grand trading room of the Merchants' Exchange, located between Wall Street and the north side of Exchange Place. As he proceeded, he nodded to many of the traders and others who found it profitable to do business in that massive building. Being preeminent among them, Thaddeus knew many of them by name, and almost every one of them knew him. As was his custom, he paused in the central rotunda to contemplate the fifteen-foot white marble statue of Alexander Hamilton, which stood in the center of the rotunda, underneath the building's dome. *A wonderful image of a remarkable man,* he thought. *People call it a marvel of the new world, and little wonder—I never tire of looking at it myself.*

Another man was also gazing at it. When he saw Bender doing the same, he walked over to him and said, "A handsome statue, is it not, sir, particularly in view of the fact that Alexander Hamilton was born a bastard."

"True enough," Thaddeus replied, "and yet he became the father of the American commercial system."

"And this in spite of his being orphaned at an early age," said the man.

"Which all goes to show what you can do if you were born brilliant," Thaddeus said.

"Well Mr. Bender, you ought to know."

Thaddeus looked at him closely. "Excuse me sir," he said, "do I know you?"

"Probably not," said the man. "My name is not important, but *your name is.* I congratulate you sir." He tipped his hat to Thaddeus, who bowed in return.

Still glowing from this encounter, Thaddeus headed toward the street. As he walked past the tall Corinthian columns, he thought, *what a building! What a fitting temple to our commercial progress—with its two-foot thick walls, it will last forever! How lucky I am to belong here! I've come a long way from that collateral-free loan that got me started.*

At that moment, he noticed, out of the corner of his eye, a tall thin man, dressed completely in black, bowing to him. Thaddeus turned to face him. "Good day, sir," said Thaddeus, "do I know you?"

"You don't recognize me right now," said the man in black, "but in time, you will."

"Will I truly?" said Thaddeus.

"Certainement, Monsieur. Au revoir." And with that, the man in black disappeared into the crowd.

Thaddeus followed his departure with a puzzled look, then shrugged off the encounter. *Life is too short,* he thought, *and I am too busy to bother with such eccentrics.* And so Thaddeus, like many of the traders needing a snack, repaired to Delmonico's Café, close by on 23 William Street. As he walked in, a waiter said, "good morning Mr. Bender. The usual?"

"Please," said Thaddeus, and the waiter immediately brought him a cup of coffee and a cruller. Whereupon in walked Cornelius Van Wyk Lawrence, the first directly elected Mayor of New York. The Mayor, a popular figure, was greeted warmly by many patrons in the place, and he acknowledged their greetings by tipping his hat to all. But after paying these respects, the Mayor headed directly toward Thaddeus' table.

Flames

The two men greeted each other with especial warmth; they were evidently good friends. "Thaddeus!" cried Lawrence, "you're just the man I've been looking for!"

"Am I?" said Thaddeus, "This is a pleasure indeed, Mr. Mayor—a pleasure, and an honor. But to what do I owe it? Wait—before you tell me your errand—may I treat you to what I'm having?" And before Lawrence had a chance to reply, Thaddeus called to the waiter: "A coffee and cruller for my good friend, the Mayor!"

"You're too good," said the Mayor.

"Just how good I am we'll both learn when I hear your errand, Cornelius."

"Thaddeus, I need your advice."

"On what?"

"On a matter of policy."

"Policy? Don't you have crowds of hangers-on to advise you on that?"

"Yes, and that's just the problem. Instead of advising me on what's good for the city, they have in mind mainly what's good for their constituents."

"I'd probably do no better: I'd advise you principally on what's good for business and banking."

"Which at least is different from the advice I'm getting now."

"I daresay. A Jacksonian Democrat like you can't appear to be partial to bankers, now can he? Personally, I like you a lot, Cornelius—always have. But I know on which side my bread is buttered, so I stood in one of those endless lines in the driving rain—and voted *Whig*, not Democrat."

"Good for you. I might have voted Whig myself—if I hadn't been nominated by Tammany Hall."

Paul R. Cooper

"I wonder why you accepted the nomination."

"So do I. This city is ungovernable."

Thaddeus put his finger to his lips: the waiter was approaching with the Mayor's snack.

"Giuseppe!" the Mayor cried to the waiter, "I haven't seen you in months! How is Marco?"

"Growing like weed, as they say over here. He wants to be waiter, like me—take my job, maybe!"

"Nobody will ever replace you, Giuseppe," the Mayor assured him, "you're too good at what you do. And how is the wife—Felìcita, if I remember right?"

"Felìcita? She's a-blooming! Another bambino on the way."

"Another one? Truly? But of course, Giuseppe—what did I tell you? You're really good at what you do!"

And as the Mayor and the waiter continued their small talk, Thaddeus reflected that the one really good at what he did was Mayor Lawrence, who seemed to be on a first name basis with almost everyone in the city. If anybody could govern New York, it ought to be Cornelius...and yet, was even *he* finding it ungovernable?

After the waiter was safely away, Thaddeus said: "I agree with your estimation of the city."

"We agree on that, at least," said the Mayor. "Any place else would be easier to deal with. *There,* for example," he said, pointing to a primitive rendering of a Tuscan landscape, one of many such works adorning the walls of the Café. "Sometimes I'd much rather be *there* than here."

"After your first week," said Thaddeus, "you'd be bored silly."

Flames

The Mayor laughed. "After the first three days, probably."

"All right," said Thaddeus. "Now that we've established that you're here and not there, tell me: what particular problem has sent you to me?"

"The firemen."

"The firemen?!"

"Shhh!" This time, it was the Mayor's turn to quiet the conversation. In a hushed voice, he continued: "Yes, the firemen. Doubtless they're stout fellows and brave. But each fire company thinks it's a law unto itself."

"Well, they're volunteers."

"Precisely; each man donates his time, and would like to think of himself as a hero—and who would say nay? The citizens treat them *all* like heroes; and they do owe them a lot; no doubt about it. But I hate to tell you: sometimes buildings burn while fire companies brawl to see which of them will have the honor of putting out the fire—and that's carrying individualism too far!"

"I agree. So do you want a businessman's solution to the problem?"

"I'd come to nowhere else for it."

"Change the system. Let the firemen *not* be volunteers, but paid professionals, owing their allegiance not to their fraternity—which is what each individual fire company amounts to—but to the *city*, which is paying their salaries. And let the chief salary go to a fire commissioner—someone who knows not only how to put out a fire, but also how to run a large organization. That way you'd no longer have an assortment of individual fire companies, you'd have one great, professional fire *department,* and you'd have accountability for its supervision. And do you know what that means?"

"Your taxes would go up, Thaddeus."

"I'd pay them willingly, so long as the money went to fighting fires, and not lining the pockets of politicians."

"*And* there'd be riots in the streets."

"Really—over that?"

"Of course! Nowadays, New Yorkers riot over everything! We just put down the stone cutter's riot—"

"But that was over a substantial issue."

"They don't *need* a substantial issue, Thaddeus. There were riots right after I was elected. They went on for three days! You remember—I was wounded!"

"The issue there may have been more substantial than you're willing to admit, Cornelius, what with your Tammany boys trying to block the Whigs from voting."

"I had nothing to do with that."

"I didn't say you had."

"They were *not my Tammany boys.*" The Mayor's fingers started drumming the red and white checkered tablecloth.

"All right, I misspoke. *The* Tammany boys."

"Much better. And I would remind you, Thaddeus, that good policy is easier to propose than to do."

"Of course. Neither of us may live to see business-like measures adopted here, but the sooner they are, Cornelius, the safer this city will be. Your job is to plant this in people's minds, so the seed can grow. There: I've given you the best advice I know how. What do you think?"

"I have an idea," said the Mayor: "Maybe I should go back to my old firm—Hicks, Lawrence & Co. That auction house made me some millions. If some are good, maybe more are better. "

"Interesting!" Thaddeus said. But if you go back to auctioneering, who would be mayor?"

"You! You'd love it."

"I'd hate it. As Mayor, I'd have to answer to all the citizens of this city. But as merchant banker, all I have to answer to are my customers, my stockholders, and my daughter."

"Your daughter? Does she expect more than the usual?"

"Well, if she had her way, I'd act always like a true Christian, and give my employees a living wage—that sort of thing."

"I should hope you would. But what happens if you fall short of being a true Christian? I don't see you being overly generous to your help."

"I'm not. My employees are there to deliver me more value than it costs me to hire them. If I can't make a decent profit on them, why should I bother with them? "

"That doesn't sound particularly Christian to me," the Mayor said.

"I don't pretend that it is. I can only hope that my daughter will be satisfied to find me an honest man."

"Then Thaddeus, you'd better become honest," said the Mayor.

His friend gave him a very wounded look.

"Cheer up, Thaddeus. I was just joking, of course."

"Of course, Cornelius. Of course."

Flames

Seven
Two visits

On Sunday afternoon, Sean, Emily, and Beatrice were standing on the street's edge, visiting the ruins of a couple of adjoining buildings recently burned out. "We fought this one two weeks ago," Sean told Emily. "It started in the house to the right. But because the two houses were separated only by a party wall, the fire spread quickly to the other."

"What's a party wall?" Emily asked.

"It's a single wall that two buildings share. They're cheaper to build that way, but very unsafe."

A surge of indignation animated Emily. "There should be a law against party walls," she said.

"In faith, there should be, Miss Emily, but there isn't. Yet even if there were one, it wouldn't do much good. People ignore what laws there are. The three-story law, for instance."

"What's that?"

"It limits building heights to three stories, because our fire engines can't pump water much higher. Not reliably. So that law makes sense, right? But everyone ignores it. They build 'em as high as they want."

"Really!" cried Emily, temporarily forgetting that her own home was four stories high.

"I'm afraid so. These houses here were four stories high, and we had to let 'em burn down to three stories before our water streams could reach 'em. And now what's left standing? Just this one blackened door. It's strange. This door used to open onto somebody's parlor, and now look what it opens onto—a lot of charred ruins."

"It's...awful," said Emily. "Did the families get out safely? Was anyone burned?"

"Nobody."

"Thank Heavens," she breathed.

"But in the house to the right," continued Sean, "a beam fell on one of our men—Tommy. They had to take his leg off—what with the gangrene and all."

Emily was feeling a little faint, and took a small side step to avoid falling.

Beatrice, ever vigilant, came up to her from behind and seized her shoulders to steady her: "You all right, child?"

"I'm fine; I'll be fine," said Emily; "thanks, Beatrice. You can let go now; I'm fine, now."

Beatrice withdrew her hands.

"I shouldn't have gone on like this," Sean said. "Forgive me. Let's talk about something else."

"Don't you dare talk about anything else," said Emily. "If firemen like you are brave enough to face these things, then hearing about them is the least I can do. Please go on."

There was a brief silence.

"Please, Mr. Dougherty, what were you going to say?" Emily asked. "Don't worry about me. I want to hear *every word.*"

"Well, Miss Emily, I was going to say that I keep thinking about the builders of these two houses. They had to choose: should they do it the right way, or the cheap way? Should they obey the law—or pile on the profit? They probably didn't think of the cripple their shoddy work might produce, much less the two families burned out of their homes. Or if it did cross their minds, they may have thought: *It's not our problem.*"

Flames

"I'm glad you think enough of me to tell me the truth," Emily said, "though hearing it makes me want to cry."

"It makes *me* want to thrash someone," said Sean. As far as I'm concerned, unregulated self interest does *not* contribute to the public good—Adam Smith notwithstanding."

"Adam Smith?"

"The Scottish philosopher—died forty-five years ago. He wrote *The Wealth of Nations*."

"You've read that?" she said.

"When I was a boy, a Monsignor took me under his wing and taught me to read, and gave me free rein in his personal library. I read everything I could get my hands on. I wish you could have seen what he had in there—Jonathan Swift, Daniel Defoe, even translations of Greek Myth and Roman Comedy—many of those books on the Roman Index. But he encouraged me, thinking I'd grow up to be a Priest. I thought so too—until our family came here about ten years ago. Since then I've seen the most scurrilous behavior parading as Christian piety. It would make me sick if I dwelt on it."

There was a brief silence. Then Emily said, "I don't blame you for feeling that way. I think I haven't paid enough attention to these things."

"In a way I'm glad you haven't, Miss Emily. They'd disturb your peace and make you angry, too."

"There's a lot of anger in this world," said Beatrice, "and much of it is hidden. But in time that hidden anger will erupt like pus from an abscess. Then watch out."

Sean and Emily looked at her, startled.

"That very well might happen," Sean said, "if Heaven directs it. Still, we can all cheer up a little: in less than two months, these ruins will be gone, and a new pair of houses erected, with new families moved in. New Yorkers work fast, and life goes on, and merciful heavens, I'm still alive. And always I'm thinking, how precious it is to be breathing the air! And if there's a faint smell of ash in it, it reminds me of how lucky I am to be breathing at all—and how lucky I am, Miss Emily, to be standing next to a pretty girl like you."

Emily's face flushed, and she cast her gaze demurely downward. Then she said, "I don't know about that, Mr. Dougherty, but I do know you are better read than I am."

"I doubt that's true, but if it is, I hope you won't hold it against me," he said.

It was late afternoon when the door to Miss Sarah Cunningham's door opened to reveal Miss Cunningham herself, greeting her visitor, Emily Bender. "How lovely to see you again, Emily; it's been far too long! Please come in; we have, as my father would say, tea and cakes at the ready."

Soon Emily and her hostess were seated. Sarah was radiant. "Well, it's happened," she said, "Edward and I are officially engaged. He gave me this ring—isn't it beautiful?"

"Yes it is," Emily murmured, "it must have been very expensive."

"Edward wouldn't tell me what it cost, but I gather it was very dear. But Edward said I'm worth it. I really doubt that I am, but who am I to tell Edward that? Poor boy, he was so nervous waiting to see my father, and yet when it was time to go into that study, he squared his shoulders and looked so manly walking in...well, they were in there for a half an hour, and I waited outside; I could scarcely breathe. Then the door opened, and Edward came out looking so relieved! He ran to me, embraced and kissed me, and I don't know how long *that*

60

went on—when you're in ecstasy, you don't watch the clock—but when I finally came up for air, I saw that my father had been standing there all the time, grinning in the doorway; he had seen the whole thing! But I was so excited that I forgot to be embarrassed—well, *almost* forgot...but it doesn't matter. We're to be married, the date is set, the invitations are being printed—of course you're getting one, Emily, you and your father...and my mother and I are working on so many plans, my head is spinning with them! I wonder if anybody ever survives getting married! Well of course they do; if our parents' marriages hadn't worked, you and I wouldn't be sitting here right now—as proof that people survive these things. Oh! I've been chattering like a magpie; I've nearly talked your head off! Please forgive me!

"No, please...nothing to forgive," murmured Emily, "I enjoyed hearing it...I love seeing you so happy. You were saying...you were in ecstasy?"

"Must have been—I was quite beyond myself."

"Ecstasy—it must be a wonderful feeling."

Sarah went to Emily and sat next to her on the couch. "Oh, Emily," she said, "how thoughtless of me to go and on about it, while you...but don't worry. All this will happen to you too some day, then you'll know how it feels."

"Do you really think so?" Emily said. "I wonder."

Flames

Eight

Oh my poor, sentimental little boy!

It was high noon in Bloomingdale: Benjamin and his mother were strolling in their carefully landscaped English Garden. His mother asked, "So you're no longer seeing Miss Stevens?"

"No, mother. It was a relief to sever that tie."

"In spite of her father being the Colonel?"

"*Because* of it! Every time I saw her, I felt she was giving me a full dress inspection, scrutinizing every move of mine for perfect execution. I never even got close to kissing her. I think she was waiting for her father to issue the command, "by the numbers, *kiss!*""

"*Is* there such a command in the Military?"

"If it regimented love that way, I'd leave it, and find a better path to glory."

"Oh, my poor, sentimental little boy!"

"You surprise me. I thought you'd be pleased I broke off with Claire Stevens."

"You know I am. You were wasting your time with her—as you would be with any young woman other than Katherine Greene. She's young, nice looking, well educated, rich, and very devoted to you."

"I grant you—she's all of that."

"Then what's the problem? Is it that *I* want it—is that what's holding you back? And you're saying no *just to spite me?*"

Benjamin said, "Let's just say that growing up with Katherine as I have, I've come to look on her as a sister. We played in the mud, together! That's *also* true."

"*Also* true is it? Spiteful, thankless boy! You don't deserve any loving advice from me, but I'll give it to you, anyway: Katherine Greene, in case you haven't noticed, has cleaned up since, and the looks she gives you are anything but sisterly. But of course you haven't seen it. Anything so close to home, you think, scarcely merits your attention."

"I'll try to look more closely, next time."

"See that you do. For Heaven's sake, Benjamin: *grow up.*"

Benjamin sighed. "Yes, mother, I'll try."

"Not good enough, Benjy: you've said 'I'll try' countless times. It won't do. This time, you really have got to *pay more attention.*"

Flames

Nine

More riots and turmoil

Thaddeus was enjoying a snack at Delmonico's Café in the early afternoon, when in walked Cornelius Lawrence, as before. After their usual effusions of bonhomie, the Mayor sat down at Thaddeus' table. "Thaddeus," Lawrence began, "am I looking peaked, drawn, out of sorts?"

"No more than usual, since you took office."

"That's a wonder. I haven't slept for days; I've barely eaten—which reminds me, Thaddeus: aren't you going to offer me my usual coffee and cruller?"

"Of course, of course, how churlish of me to forget, Mr. Mayor."

"Thaddeus: to all and sundry I may be Mr. Mayor, but to you, I hope, I'm Cornelius."

"But of course! Waiter," he called, "will you bring Cornelius here his usual coffee and cruller?"

"My dear Thaddeus, you seem ironic and distant today. Have I done something to offend you? "

"Heavens no, Cornelius, except that you've just suppressed the only riots that could have proved useful to me."

"I presume you mean the abolitionist riots?"

"What else? If the Tappan brothers want to hold abolitionist meetings, their souls may benefit, but business will suffer. Conversely, if the rioters want to *discourage* the Tappans and their like—by destroying their property and shaking them up a little—they may be steeping their souls in sin, but business will flourish. Couldn't you have let the rioters do a little more damage before calling in the 27th regiment, the New York First Division, and the Calvary?"

"Are you joking, Thaddeus? In addition to attacking the Bowery Theatre, and wreaking havoc in Five Points, they devastated Lewis Tappan's home, stormed the Chatham Street Chapel, the Laight Street Church, and broke into the Reverend's house! What more turmoil would you have?"

"Well, Arthur Tappan's warehouse is still intact; they managed only to pelt it with stones. If you had given them a little more time, maybe they could have succeeded in setting it afire—or maybe even blowing it up."

"Good God! I never thought I'd hear you speak in favor of mob rule, Thaddeus."

"I'm not, really. I hope you know I'm joking. But still, in every joke there's a kernel of truth. And mine is that the Tappan brothers...have got to be stopped—*all* abolitionists have got to be stopped. Slavery is the economic linchpin of this city. Taking it away spells disaster."

"Especially for cotton trading operations like yours, which depend on the success of southern plantations."

"Not only my operation—every business in New York would suffer if slavery were abolished, and some would go out of business altogether. And the damned thing is...the damned thing is that the abolitionists have it *right*; they're absolutely correct: slavery—like much else of business—is immoral." Thaddeus' elegantly booted foot began tapping the wide-board floor. "You can fancy dance around it all you want," he said, "but the truth is, slavery is a huge wrong. And all you need do is persuade enough people in this country of that fact, and you've got a civil war on your hands. That's why it's better to do business as usual and let the issue develop naturally."

Flames

"Whatever that means."

"You know what it means."

"Truly I don't, Thaddeus. But let me ask, what does your daughter think of your business?"

Thaddeus' eyes darted nervously about. The Mayor picked up on this immediately: "She thinks *that little* of it?"

"She doesn't know what it is—not really."

"Is that a fact?"

"She thinks I make loans merely for local real estate, and for other northern business interests. She thinks that the only commerce I've had with slave owners was before she was born."

"Where'd she get that idea?"

"That was the tale I told her. And as soon as the lie was out of my mouth, I regretted it. But she was so relieved to hear that story that I couldn't bring myself to unsay it. And every passing day makes it harder to tell her the truth. I'm sorry I lied to her, and to ease my conscience, I tell myself that my support of slavery is indirect only—that I have no contact with the slavers themselves—though there are plenty in New York who have tried to get me involved."

"Well, that is something."

"A very small something. I don't think it will impress Emily when she learns the truth. Which has to happen, sooner or later—and I'm afraid sooner."

Lawrence said, "Thaddeus, maybe it's better your daughter learn the truth sooner, so you can live your life without this turmoil inside you."

"I apologize for unburdening myself to you this way."

"Nothing to apologize for. And don't worry, your secrets are safe with me."

"I know it," Thaddeus said.

"Shall we meet next week, as usual?"

"By all means. Let people talk."

"They're already talking," said the Mayor.

"Are they, Cornelius? What are they saying?"

"That I'm coming to you for interest-free loans—in exchange for political influence."

"Ain't politics wonderful?"

"You could always get into it. I could find you a spot."

Thaddeus shook his head decisively. "No thank you. I've got problems enough as it is." He raised his cup partly to drain the last few drops of coffee remaining in it, but also, almost unconsciously, for the comfort of hiding behind it while he drank. Having finished the last drop, he began to lower the cup but paused in this action when he saw, as he looked over the cup, the man in black, the Frenchman, sitting many tables away. The man was gazing at him, and when he saw that Thaddeus now returned his gaze, he allowed his ashen pallor to express a wan smile, and he raised his own cup in a funereal salute. Now thoroughly puzzled and a bit uneasy, Thaddeus returned the salute with his own cup, then placed it down on the table and deliberately looked away and sought the Mayor's attention. "Cornelius..." he began.

"What's the matter, Thaddeus? What's wrong? You seem so grave, of a sudden."

"Cornelius, there's a man in this restaurant dressed completely in black," said Thaddeus, never for a second taking his eyes away from the Mayor. "Do you see him?"

"No. Where is he?"

Thaddeus turned to point him out. "He's over...well, he *was* over..."

Flames

But the man in black had gone.

Flames

Ten
Yes, I do

At mid afternoon on Sunday, somewhere on South Street, near the Old Slip, the forest of tall masts that had overseen the slaughter of Joe Simon now looked down at Emily and Sean walking hand in hand under the canopy of bowsprits, with Beatrice following at a respectful distance. "I used to be down here all the time," said Sean, "but now I come only when one of our ships comes in, which is often enough since business is good, thanks be to God."

"A lot of the Irish work here?" Emily asked.

"Sure—wherever muscle power is needed, you'll find us. But it's not all Irish. You find some English and Dutch workers as well."

"And Negroes, too?"

"Not many. The Irish here resent them because—they say—the Negroes bring down the wages by workin' for less. That's what they say. I got cousins who would as soon burn a black man as look at him."

"Oh!" she cried.

"Sorry. I shouldn't have mentioned it."

"Yes you should. If it's true, you needn't be afraid to tell me. I'm old enough to hear about things."

"You sure?"

"Absolutely."

They walked briefly, in silence. Then Emily said, "you have cousins who would as soon burn a black man as look at him?"

"Yes."

71

"Burn him—literally?"

"I'm afraid so."

"Horrible! It's hard to imagine that people could think that way."

"Well, *I* used to think that way—before I met Arthur Tappan, that is. He and his brother have got up an abolitionist movement here in this city, and they have meetings all over the place. He's a godly man, is Arthur Tappan, and he starts every work day with some prayers, and he encourages the men to attend the antislavery meetings. And I've been goin'; he's quite converted me. So I no longer talk like my cousins. I know it's wrong."

"It certainly is."

"I'm glad I have your approval," said Sean, dropping her hand, and walking a little ahead of her.

"You always have my approval, Mr. Dougherty," she said, catching up to him, and taking back his hand. *What a stupid thing to say—that he has my approval! I better say something more sensible, quick!* "Is Beatrice in danger, walking down here?"

"Oh no—not while I'm nearby. And also, she's not doing any work down here—unless chaperoning you counts as work."

"Oh no—no work at all. Her presence is symbolic."

"Of what?"

"Of the fact that someone cares for me, Mr. Dougherty, and is looking out for me."

"But that would be me, wouldn't it? I'd ask if your Da trusted me, but I'll bet he doesn't even know I exist, does he?"

"Well...no, he doesn't. I haven't told him yet."

"I thought not."

"But I will…soon."

"I hope so," he said. Then with a voice noticeably raised in volume, he added, "But meanwhile, maybe it's time to leave Beatrice at home? You'll feel a lot more grown up without her tagging along—as if you weren't grown enough to think for yourself."

"I already think for myself quite well, thank you very much."

In his normal voice he remarked, "You've grown up a lot since we met at the race."

"I was more grown up then than I let on. I got into the habit of acting younger than I am; I liked how people treated me. But now that I've been with you awhile…"

"You want to act your age?"

She looked up at him, smiling, and murmured, "Yes, I do."

That evening, in her bedroom, Emily was sitting, brushing her long, auburn hair while Beatrice attended her, standing. "He said I'd feel a lot more grown up without you tagging along. Did you hear him say that?"

"It was hard not to. You were right next to him, yet he spoke loud enough to make sure I heard every word. It sounded like he *wanted* me to hear it."

"That's what I thought, too. But why would he want you to hear what he was saying?"

"Well, what do *you* think, darlin'?"

"Maybe he hoped you'd persuade me to leave you at home? Which would be as if he didn't trust me to make up my own mind, and was treating me like a child."

"It would also mean that he wants very much to be alone with you, and will do whatever it takes to get there."

"Should I be worried? If I were alone with him, would I be safe?"

"Do you *want* to be safe?"

"Yes of course—but not...*too* safe."

"Not *too* safe?"

"Part of me is afraid of him—and part of me is very...*excited*." She laughed, nervously. "He *is* a very exciting man, don't you think?"

"What do *I* think? Me personally?" Beatrice smiled. "That's neither here nor there. It's what *you* think that's important."

"Well, what I think is...that if I were truly safe I'd of course be reassured—but, to be honest, I'd be a little disappointed."

"What are you going to tell your father?"

"How do you know I'm going to tell him anything? He doesn't have to know everything I do—or with whom. And if he asks, you don't have to tell him you're no longer going with me."

"And so mislead him all the more? Wouldn't that be one too many lies on my part?"

"I suppose so. It's just that it's hard to get up the nerve to face Daddy sometimes."

A few moments later, she knocked on the door of her father's home office and began to open it even before she heard Thaddeus calling, "come on in, Emily."

74

Flames

She entered full of purpose, and said: "I need to talk with you, Father."

"So, go ahead, talk."

"What I want to say is..." She broke off in mid-sentence. What *did* she want to tell him? That she wanted to leave Beatrice at home, certainly, but there was a lot more, and she wondered if this was the time for it.

"Yes?" said Thaddeus, "what you wanted to say is...what? I'm all ears." Thaddeus smiled, encouragingly.

"Father, I've been thinking..." She broke off again, and went to the Tudor-styled windows, whose warped complexities had often provided her with something to study in moments like these when she wasn't quite sure of what to say to him.

Thaddeus, long familiar with this behavior, waited patiently.

After a few moments of window gazing, she turned to her father and said, "I'd prefer Beatrice not accompany me everywhere I go. I don't need her anymore."

Thaddeus regarded his daughter with a grave smile. He'd been expecting this request for some time.

"Sit down, why don't you." He patted his lap. "Here, perhaps?"

"Not this time," said Emily, who sat in her chair.

"Oho, grown up now, are we?"

"I hope so," Emily said. "Father, I want your permission to leave the house without Beatrice."

"Do you feel you need my permission?"

"I'd feel better if I had it."

"I'm not so sure *I* would. It may sound crazy, but I believe that your mother died because of my negligence."

Paul R. Cooper

"Oh no, Daddy!"

"I'm afraid it *is* so. Against my better judgment, I let her accompany me to Savannah, where she died giving birth to you. I vowed then to be more careful with you than I was with her. Beatrice accompanies you because *I* feel better that way."

Emily rose and went to Thaddeus. "Father, I'm the only student in Mrs. Okill's school who has to put up with a full-time chaperone. They make fun of me because of it—especially Margaret, who wonders if Beatrice will be in the bedroom chaperoning me, even on my wedding night!"

Thaddeus stiffened, and spoke very quietly in a tone he reserved for matters of the utmost gravity: "She shouldn't insult us." A faint smile played on his lips, a smile that Emily knew only too well, along with the words that usually followed: "No one should do that. Not to us. There are consequences."

"Oh, no," cried Emily, leaning toward him, "it's not like that. Margaret was only joking, she meant no harm; no need for consequences, Daddy!" And Emily, almost by instinct, placed a restraining hand on Thaddeus' right arm. "It's just that I felt she spoke the truth; that's why it stung so much. I *am* too old for a chaperone."

"Hm. I thought you liked Beatrice."

"I *love* her. But the time comes when we have to separate from the ones we love—a little, at first."

"And that time has come for you and Beatrice?"

"Yes."

"And for you and me?"

"Oh no, Daddy, not for a long time. And if you give me a little freedom, that time will come for us later, rather than sooner."

76

Flames

"That sounds like a very grown up thing to say."
"I was hoping it would."

Flames

Eleven

You'll know.

It was Sunday afternoon, and Sean was showing Emily the first floor of Arthur Tappan's store and warehouse, where he worked. He pointed to the rear of the first floor. "All the goods we receive come in by way of the entrance back there on Water Street, because it's closer to the docks."

"So that should make it easier."

"It would be easier yet if the back door were wider."

"Why don't you suggest that to Mr. Tappan?"

"There must be a reason for using the door as it is; Mr. Tappan's a smart man. Besides, who am I to suggest that sort of thing to him?"

"You're his Shop Floor Steward, that's who!"

"Yes, but only newly promoted from dock hand and stock boy. I try to keep my mouth shut."

"He gave you the key to the place, so he must trust you a lot."

"I try to live up to it. I have to: you see that little office over there?" Sean pointed to a small office situated right in the center of the warehouse floor, and surrounded by low partitions. "That's where Mr. Tappan works, right where he can keep an eye on all our clerks—a score or more of them—and an eye on *me*. He doesn't miss a thing. If a bundle is received without proper examination, or if it's stored in the wrong place, or if an order goes missing, or is shipped at the wrong time, or by the wrong route, or to the wrong address, it's my fault."

"A heavy responsibility! Do you lose sleep over it?"

"Some times. But mostly I'm too tired to lose sleep over much."

"This is really impressive! Too bad Beatrice is not here to see it."

"Why *isn't* she here? I thought you were going to bring her, as usual."

"Not after the speech you made near the docks, last Sunday."

"I have that power over you, do I?"

"If I said yes, would it please you?"

"It would please any man to have power over his girl. And yet...I wouldn't want so much power that she didn't have power over *me*."

"Do I have power over you?"

"More than I know how to tell you."

"Oh!" she breathed, pleased, but disconcerted. She looked for a way to change the subject. "That's an interesting platform over there—it looks like a stage."

This platform was thirty inches high and set against a wall. On the floor in front it were various bins containing umbrellas, handkerchiefs, scarves, and other items made from silk and sundry exquisite fabrics. On top of the platform itself were wooden frames to display to their fullest advantage the fabrics themselves. At one end of the platform some stairs allowed easy access to the platform's top.

"It *is* like a stage," said Sean, "to display some of our stock to customers who come here in person. In the bins below we keep the umbrellas, handkerchiefs, and so forth, and up above on those frames you can see some of the fabrics we like to show off. Occasionally, a customer will want to make a special order—for his wife, let's say. And when the wife comes with him, she'll want to get up on the stage and get a close look, and maybe drape the fabric on herself, and ask her husband if the colors are right for her."

"Does she use those little stairs over there?"

"Sure."

"May I?

"Of course."

So she did, quickly, and walked to where the fabrics were displayed on the frameworks. "Now I'm a very fancy lady," she said, and I'll just see if the fabric on this frame is right for me." She lifted from the framework a silk brocade in azure and crimson and held it to her face. "Do these colors suit me?"

"You would look beautiful in that," he said, "but then, you'd look beautiful in *anything.*"

"I think not," she said. "And I think I'll be very picky today, so that nothing will suit me. I'll just come down," she said, starting to walk toward the stairs.

"No, no!" he cried, "you don't need the stairs. I'll help you down." He extended his arms to her, and she paused, plainly deciding whether to let him.

"May I?" he asked.

She thought a moment, then quietly said, "all right," and he reached up to clasp her waist, and then, very slowly, without apparent effort, he lifted her, drew her to him, and even more slowly lowered her to the ground, their bodies almost touching. Her hands were on his arms, and her eyes were fixed on his.

"You are so strong," she whispered.

His face drew close to hers and, after a brief hesitation, he kissed her gently. He drew back a little, gazing at her. "You are an angel," he said, then drew her close and kissed her again, more warmly. He drew back again, and she looked up at him.

"Are all firemen like you?"

"Oh my love," he cried, "I have no idea!" Then he kissed her again—this time passionately. She threw her arms around him, drowning in a tide of feeling.

In one of the many taverns dotting Manhattan, there was a table so far in the rear that after dark, the available light barely reached it. Most of the tavern's patrons probably didn't notice in that dark corner a small ceramic statuette of the Buddha, probably a souvenir of somebody's voyage to Asia. If its serene smile was meant to influence its beholders to detach themselves from their cravings, it was a signal failure in the case of Sean Dougherty, who, at around 9 PM, was sitting at this table of shadows, directing a melancholy gaze on a shot glass of whiskey, from which he had taken only one sip. His bleak meditation was interrupted by a short, rotund young man who stroke briskly up to his table. "You look like you could use some company," said the stranger. May I join you?"

"It's a free country," said Sean morosely, "so I doubt I could stop you."

Ignoring the hint, the stranger sat down across from Sean, and ordered a carafe of wine from one of the pretty waitresses working at the place. "Can I get something for you?" he asked Sean.

"No thanks. I still have some."

"The name is Egmont," the stranger said, "That's right: Egmont, but my friends call me Eg. Which doesn't bother me—my name may be Eg, but I won't break, ha, ha!"

"Glad to hear it."

Flames

"And now that I've introduced myself, may I know *your* name?"

"You can call me Sean."

"Well then, Sean, what's troubling you?"

"I don't want to be rude or anything, but is it any of your business?"

"Oh, I think so, I think so. For I'll ask you, do you know the expression, 'misery loves company?' Well, *I'm* perfectly miserable," said Egmont cheerfully, "perfectly miserable. And seeing that you may be just a bit miserable, too, I figure we can drown in our sorrows together, and as we're drowning, be a little less miserable as we go down together, ha, ha!"

After a moment of looking at Egmont with frank disbelief, Sean finally said, "and what may be making *you* miserable, if you don't mind my asking?"

"I love an audience, so I don't mind at all. I spend my days standing up in an office, calculating sums and differences. I'm a Computer: that's my title—my *role*, really. I compute things, and what I do all day is mainly add and subtract stuff. Other workers in my office get to talk to people—*they* get the dialogue—but not me! They just hand me lists of numbers, and I add 'em or subtract 'em—whatever they need. They write their needs down on paper; they don't even waste a spoken word on me! So I go ahead and compute. I pretend to figure it out on paper, but the truth is, I do it all in my head. I'm a freak—I never make a mistake. Which means that to promote me, they'd have to be fools—*fools*, I tell you! I'll never earn enough money to marry and have a family. I'm stuck where I am. Not only that, sometimes my boss will give me extra assignments for after hours—sometimes really outlandish things—and I'm bound to do 'em if I want to keep my job.

83

Almost every night I'm at his beck and call; there's only one night a month I can call my own—I call it *freedom night,* ha, ha!"

"It does sound like a miserable life," Sean said, "but you seem so jolly about it. I wonder why?"

"Because *tonight* is freedom night! Tonight I get to *talk* to people—people like you. Or, if there are no customers to talk to, well, just look at those waitresses—they're always willing to pick up a little extra business upstairs, if you understand me. And they give you complete service, *complete* service—if you know what I mean."

"I'm afraid to ask what you mean."

"What I mean is, that if you'd like, they'll *talk* to you while you're doin' it. Along with everything else, you can get in some dialogue, if you want. They might be just the thing for you—take that frown off your face and make you feel better."

"No, no," said Sean, "that's not my deal at all."

"Aha! Not that way inclined, are you?"

"I'm no queer, if that's what you mean. No, I have a girl friend, and my problem is that I get to see her mainly on Sundays. I've got a few days more to wait, and it's hard."

"Ah, cheer up. When you do see her, she'll give you all you want, so you won't need the waitresses; I understand you."

"You don't understand me at all, Mr. Egg, or whatever the hell your name is. I don't like what you're driving at. My girl is as pure as the driven snow, and she deserves a man who'll respect that."

"And you always do, is that what you're telling me?"

"Well this past Sunday, we kissed for the first time, and I have to admit I was carried away—enough so that...had she been willing…I might have let things take their natural course. But it's glad I am that we didn't. I want to do things right, and she deserves no less from me. She needs a man who'll protect her from every sort of harm, and I want to be that man."

"The perfect suitor—an admirable role! And does she return your affections?"

"Well." Sean grimaced. "I would have thought so—but she hasn't told her father about me."

"You mean he doesn't even *know?* The plot thickens!"

"Whatever that means. No, Mr. Egg, according to her, he doesn't know yet. She keeps promising to tell him, but she hasn't yet. I think she's afraid to."

"Why would that be?"

"Because her father is as rich as Croesus, while I am as poor as a church mouse. I'm in a different world."

"I suppose you would be—working as a warehouse Shop Floor Steward."

Sean gave him a sharp look. "How'd you know that? I haven't mentioned it."

"You haven't? I must have picked it up when I came in. Around here, everyone knows everyone else's business."

"Then you probably know that Emily likes me, but she feels I'm simply too poor to bring home to her father. I fear that's the simple truth of it."

"Too bad for you. Marriage to a rich girl would have quite set you up in life."

"I hate that!"

"The money?"

"No—I'm not a fool. Though her father's money, so far as I'm concerned, is tainted with blood."

"Sounds fascinating!"

"It's sordid, that's what it is. And Emily has no knowledge of it. She's really an angel. I want to be sure that I want her for her sake, and not for the sake of her father's money. It doesn't help that my Da always says, "it's just as easy to fall in love with a rich girl as it is with a poor one."

"Does your father know about Emily?"

"No—he's in Boston doing construction work. My mother knows about her but hasn't met her. That'll change. I'm bringing Emily to her soon."

"That should be an interesting scene to play out."

"To say the least. But Emily wants me to bring her. To her own father she doesn't dare bring me, but she's fine with meeting my Ma."

"How about you? Are you fine with it?"

"I'll find out, won't I?"

Late afternoon, a few days later, Sean and Emily were gingerly making their way through Five Points, avoiding the refuse, human and animal wastes on the sidewalks and streets. Ahead of them they saw some half dozen very small children who made no attempt to avoid these urban excrescences, but ran recklessly through them. Sean heard Emily's sharp intake of breath. "These kids are three or four years old," he said. "Those who make it to five will be put to work and won't have time for running through the streets—dirty as they are."

"Horrible," she said. "Why would anyone want to bring children into a world like this?"

"For a lot of reasons," he replied, "one of them being that after a certain age, children can be useful. People do think like that—although at the crucial moment, the parents probably aren't doing much thinking at all—their passion has taken over."

By this time, the children had disappeared, and the couple had reached a relatively clear stretch of the street. Sean took Emily's hand. "Their world will not be ours," he said.

For a while they walked hand in hand, wordlessly.

"A penny for your thoughts," he said.

"You said something about passion taking over. Well, when you kissed me," she said, "things were spinning so...I lost track of where I was. I think you could have...done whatever you wanted. I'm glad you didn't."

"So am I," he said. "It wouldn't have been right."

"Did I disappoint you?"

"If you had said yes, that would have disappointed me."

"It won't always be this way," she said.

"Shh!" He placed his finger to his lips. "We're here."

He knocked on the door, which opened to reveal his mother. "Come in, darlin' boy," she said, "and bring your belle with you!"

His mother gave Emily an examining look, scanning from top to toe. "She's a pretty one, all right," said Megan, "I'll give you *that*, Seanie."

"Thank you, Mrs. Dougherty," murmured Emily.

"Oh, ho!" cried Sean's mother, "she speaks, too! Very promising."

"I'll thank you to treat her right, Ma—none of your high handed mockery, or I'll be upset."

"Oh, upset is it? Well, you're entitled to be upset—we *all* are. But sit yourselves down, dearies. What about some tea? *That* you're entitled to, at the very least, and I have some all ready to pour you."

Sean and Emily had in hand the two real china tea cups Megan had brought from Ireland, while Megan's own tea was in one of the four stoneware mugs she used regularly. The young couple apprehensively watched Megan take a long, considered sip before she declared, "children, it's good to see a bit o' happiness in the world now and again, and looking at you, I have to say that it's glad I am for you both, surely. But Saints preserve us, I wouldn't be doing my duty if I didn't warn you, my dear Sean: she comes from money; you do not. That's the fact. And even with all the love in the world, and all the fair minded understanding, that fact is going to bump up ugly when you least expect it, like warts on her lovely complexion. And almost every day, in one way or another, she'll be thinking of what she *could have had*, and you'll be kicking yourself for living with someone you can never measure up to. You'll see yourself as small in her eyes, and soon you'll be small in your own."

Emily and Sean gazed at each other over their tea, which remained untasted.

In Emily's bedroom at 9 PM that evening, Beatrice was brushing Emily's hair, and Emily asked, "Beatrice, should I marry Sean?"

"Honey chile, if you have to ask me that, the answer's a big fat NO. Marriage can be a thorn patch all by itself, without your adding more barbs to it."

"I was afraid you'd say that."

Flames

"Well, look, child: even if he had as much money as your father, he'd still be a Catholic and you a Methodist. Is that likely to change?"

"No."

"There you are. And as for the money part, it isn't the lack of material possessions alone which should worry you— it's that some things he's used to are going to offend you. His habits, I mean. Do you know what I'm saying?"

"I fear I do."

"You see."

"The trouble is, Beatrice, I love him. I don't know if I can live without him."

"Poor dear, that *is* trouble."

"You won't tell Father, will you?"

"Never. I swore an oath on it, and you can depend on it. But look, he hasn't proposed yet, has he?"

"No. I think he's a little shy of it."

"That's fine. He *ought* to be shy at this point. Just take your time; this is nothing to rush into."

"And then what?"

"There'll come a time when you won't have to ask me. You'll *know.*"

"Will I? What will I know?"

At that moment, they heard a fire bell in the distance.

"Listen," said Emily, "that's a fire bell. That means that soon, a lot of firemen will be risking their lives. One of them could be Sean. That's *all* I know."

Flames

Twelve
I hope he'll be so good as to tell me.

The fire bell that Emily heard was still ringing as Engine Co. No. 5 was the first of two companies to arrive at a row house fire raging near the Five Points. Since Sean's company was the first, it was entitled to use the hydrant and coordinate the activities of the second fire company. So both were captained by Sean Dougherty, who, speaking trumpet in hand, was deploying all the firefighters. They saw standing outside the house a middle aged man with his wife and son; they had just escaped. But his wife was screaming that still in the house was her baby girl; the father had been unable to get to her.

Sean shouted, "What floor?"

"The third!" cried the father. "I tried my best, but I couldn't make it!"

Sean nodded, and began to formulate orders for his men when he became conscious of a tugging at his sleeve. A young "runner"—a fourteen-year-old volunteer not part of either company—was trying to get his attention. Trying to ignore him, Sean told his men to throw up a ladder to a window on the third floor, and told Timmy to ascend it as soon as it was positioned. Then he called to the other company head, "Gabe, take over—I'm going in!" He headed for the front door, but the young volunteer kept pestering him, so Sean called again to Gabe: "Will you see what this young'un wants? I haven't time!" And Sean disappeared into the building.

Gabe said to the young volunteer, "what the hell is wrong with you? Can't you see we're trying to fight a fire?"

"I'm sorry," the lad said, "but I've been running to fires

for two years, so I can take over when a fireman gets too tired to pump."

"Fine. Do it."

"I can't right now. Nobody's tired."

"Then wait till somebody is, and don't bother me."

"But I could take that nigger's place."

"Are you crazy? That man is more than four times as strong as you. He pumps like two full grown men. Let him!"

"But he doesn't *belong* here—he's black!"

"He could be green, for all I care! Anybody who can pump like that belongs here."

At that moment, Sean appeared at the window, with the baby girl in his arms. He handed her off to Timmy, who started down the ladder with her. As soon as Timmy made it to the second floor, Sean himself got on the ladder and started descending as fast as he could. Both firemen and the baby made it safely to the ground just as the third floor collapsed into the second. While Timmy put the baby in the arms of the overjoyed parents, Sean went to the other company head, who was still being pestered. "What's going on here, Gabe?" he asked, "what does that lad want?"

The young volunteer stepped up and said, "I want to take my place on the brakes! I've been running to fires for two years, and I deserve a place! While that black bastard is new here, and anyways he doesn't belong here!"

Sean put an arm around the young volunteer's shoulders, walked aside with him, and quietly said, "Calm down, my friend, and listen: that black man is not a member of any company I know. But I'll tell you this: if he were to volunteer for *my* company, I'd take him in a heartbeat. That's how I feel about him. And if saving lives and property becomes more important to you than anything else—and I mean *anything* else—I'll feel the same way about you, too. Do you know what I'm saying?"

"You're sayin' you love niggers," said the boy, who spat, and ran off.

Gabe came up to Sean. "What did you tell that idiot?"

"Oh God! Heaven only knows. I swear that lately I've been so preoccupied I scarcely know what I'm doing half the time."

"Wounded you that bad, did it?"

"Did what?"

"Cupid's arrow."

"You know about my love life?"

"Word travels fast. Everybody knows about it."

"Then if some guy learns she loves me, I hope he'll be so good as to tell me."

Flames

Thirteen
I plan to tell him…soon

"It's kind of cold for early December," said Sean; "are you all right, Emily?"

"Pretty much. And we'll be there soon, right—out of this wind?"

"It's not too long, now," he replied

Emily and Sean were in a neighborhood not unlike where Sean's mother lived. Each was carrying a bundle: Emily had a bundle of blankets, Sean one of food. He said to Emily, "We'll be visiting the widow Gallagher this time. She's just after losing her husband in a construction accident. Bunch of bricks fell on him. They got no money." He knocked on a dilapidated door. It was opened by a young woman with a babe in arms, and a toddler hanging on to her skirts. "It's me, Mrs. Gallagher," said Sean. "Can we come in?"

The interior of the widow Gallagher's one-room home was stark, to say the least. Her few dishes, though clean, were all chipped or broken. On the hard earth floor was a straw mattress on which she and her children slept together, and a chamber pot. There was little else.

Sean said, "Mrs. Gallagher, this is my friend, Emily Bender. She got the idea of helping out, and she and I have been getting it going."

"Seanie told me about your trouble, Mrs. Gallagher, so we took the liberty of bringing you some things. Look: here's some smoked ham, some bread and cheese, and potatoes. And in this other package we brought some blankets to help keep you warm of nights."

Mrs. Gallagher's eyes filled with tears. "Thanks be to God!" she cried, "I didn't know what we were going to do! May God bless the both of you; you're so kind!" She started sobbing, and Emily put her arms around her.

"There, there, Mrs. Gallagher," she said, "we're glad to be able to help. But what a fine boy you have here! What's his name?"

"His name is Matthew, same as his Da. Looks like him, too. Spittin' image—red hair and all."

Sean knelt down. "You're getting to be a real grown up, aren't you boy?"

The lad just stared at him.

"Now, now, Matt," said his mother, "be a good boy and answer the kind gentleman."

But little Matthew said nothing.

"That's all right," said Sean, patting the youngster on the head. "The important thing, my lad, is to take care of your Ma. You're the man of the house now, don't forget. Your Ma needs you more than ever." Sean stood, and turned to Emily. "But what do you think, Emily—it's time to be takin' our leave, right?"

Emily said, "it was nice meeting you, Mrs. Gallagher. Maybe we can come back again."

"I hope so," Mrs. Gallagher said.

Sean and Emily made their way to the door, opened it, and were about to leave when little Matthew finally did pipe up: "Thank you!" he said.

Out on the street again, Emily and Sean walked half a block without saying anything. Then Sean said, "She was in tears."

"I was too," Emily said.

Flames

"Mr. Tappan would call this an example of doing God's work. That's what you did."

"That's what we *both* did," Emily said. "Without your help, this wouldn't have happened." He put his arm around her waist, and she responded in kind. "Darling," she said, I feel so close to you."

"And I, too," he said, "very close."

They continued walking, and then he said, "Does your Da know about us, yet?"

"No, but he will! I plan to tell him...soon."

"I sure hope so," he said.

Flames

Fourteen
I Really Am Miss Cone

There was no need to check the number on the door, Egmont decided, for the name of the establishment, "Cone's Custom Clothing" appeared very prominently on the sign above. He opened the door and saw, sitting behind the counter and looking up from her sewing, Nehemias' daughter Rachel, who struck him as so beautiful that he quite forgot to adopt the manic persona he usually presented to the world. "My name is Egmont Blühen," he said soberly, "and I'm looking for Nehemias Cone. Is he here?"

"No," Rachel said, "he's away on business. He won't be back for at least another hour. May I help you?"

"I was sent here today by my boss, Thaddeus Bender, to pick up his latest order."

"I'm surprised," Rachel said, resuming her sewing, "for we had sent him word three days ago that it would be at least another six before it was finished."

"So it won't be ready for another three days?"

"At the very least," said Rachel. "Perhaps he didn't receive our message?"

"Oh, he got it all right."

"Well then why on earth..."

"Probably he thought he'd be lucky, and it wouldn't hurt to try for it."

Rachel stopped sewing for a moment and looked at him. "And if Mr. Bender wanted the sun no longer to rise in the East," she said, her head tilted quizzically, "would he try for that, too?"

"Are you then as immutable as the rising of the Sun?"

"I fear the limit of my work speed is," said Rachel, resuming her sewing, "and no amount of cajoling can increase it; I'm already sewing as fast as I can—or was, until you came in. I'll tell my father you called."

"Then this interview is at an end?"

"Is there a point in prolonging it?"

"Yes: I'm enjoying myself hugely."

Rachel stopped sewing. "Hugely, sir? How extravagant! And what would be the cause of this huge enjoyment?" Her eyes were sparkling.

Egmont returned her smile. "Can't say that I know," he said. "I'll have to think about it."

Actually, Egmont didn't have to think about it; he knew the cause: here was a woman who, by the look of her, had never felt the need to be other than her own lovely self. No playacting for *her*—she *was*.

"Well, if you'll let me get back to my work, you can go away and think about it," she said. "And when you have figured it out, you can come back and tell me."

"I'll do just that," he said. "It's been a pleasure, Miss Cone. It *is* Miss Cone isn't it—or am I mistaken on that one, too? You're not someone else pretending to be Miss Cone?"

"No, I am not pretending, sir," she said with a smile that pierced him. "I really am Miss Cone."

Flames

Fifteen
A hot-house flower

"Where are we going, Seanie dear?" said Emily, "I don't think I've been in this neighborhood before."

"We're going to a revival meeting at the Free Presbyterian Chapel on Chatham Street," he said.

"I thought you were Roman Catholic."

"I'm not sure *what* I am anymore," he said, "God only knows, and maybe someday He'll let me in on it. I was raised Catholic, sure enough, but if I want to hear Mr. Tappan speak, I have to come here. But enough about me—what do you think of *this?*" he said, pointing out a large fountain of water on the way to the chapel entrance.

"It's an interesting feature for a chapel," she said.

"It's there because this place used to be a theatre," he said.

"Does your mother know you come here?"

"I doubt it."

When the couple entered the auditorium Emily gasped. "Beatrice—*she's* here!"

"Interesting," Sean said. "Normally white people and blacks don't like mixing with each other even in church. Something's up."

"Who's that bearded man she's talking to?"

"That's Mr. Tappan himself."

"Will he be preaching?"

"Oh, no. He doesn't like public speaking much. The preacher is Charles Grandison Finney. But Tappan will say *something*, you can be sure of it. And that's what I'm waiting for. Finney's good—he can convert a stone to Christianity—but he can be long winded. When he finally gets to the end of it, then you'll hear Tappan, and get some sense of the man."

Emily and Sean sat down. "How long will it take?" she asked.

"About an hour and a half. It won't be bad—you'll find Finney interesting."

But what interested Emily during the ensuing ninety minutes wasn't so much Finney's message as it was the rapture of his listeners, who really seemed to like this sort of thing. What appealed to Emily was her hand in Sean's, the mere contact of which was enough to take her out of the chapel into her world of dreams, in which Sean and she had a small cottage nestled some place in Bloomingdale, where the perfume of roses lasted all summer long, and the children ran about happily. These dreams were repeatedly interrupted by Finney's rhetorical explosions, the most passionate of which was his conclusion:

*"My friends, Jesus is calling you! And you <u>know</u> that you don't have to do anything to deserve God's love. God loves you <u>as you are!</u> Just as you are in your sins God loves you, and for you <u>just in that state</u> he gave his Son to die for you. This is what you must believe. You must think: it was <u>as I am</u> that Christ died for me; it was <u>as a sinner</u> that God loved me, and loves me still; as a sinner then I will go to Jesus, as I am, as an humble penitent, a seeking, but not deserving sinner. Will you come? Will you come now? Will you believe now? **Or make God a liar?** Oh no. Let us all come to Jesus! Amen."*

"Amen! Amen, brother!" were some of the cries coming from the audience.

Flames

"And now, dear friends," said Finney, "here is Lewis Tappan, who has rented this space so that we can present the Gospel this day. He deserves our thanks."

To the applause of the audience, Lewis Tappan strode up and said, "I'm not the most important Tappan here. That honor belongs to my brother. Arthur, will you stand and say a few words?"

Arthur Tappan stood up, did not go to the rostrum, but spoke from where he was standing, very quietly, and with great humility: "Christ died for the colored man as well as for the white man" he said. "So you and I are bound to...remove the walls blocking the colored man, and give him a chance, offer him the right hand of fellowship, do away with oppression, and treat him as a fellow citizen *here*, in the land of his birth, in the land in which we say: *all men are created equal.*"

These words were greeted with applause. Then Arthur continued: "I'd like you to meet Beatrice; she has something important to tell us."

And Beatrice rose, and in a resonant voice began: "About ten years ago I received a letter from my cousin, Dora, in Poughkeepsie. Let me read from the letter. She wrote: 'A black slave—about 20 years old—fired his master's barn, killing much livestock, and destroying much grain. They caught him, he confessed, and they condemned him to be burned to death. They tied him to the stake, and they fired the pile, but there was such a dense crowd gathered around him that the air was cut off, and the fire burned slowly, and the screams of the boy were heard for more than a mile. His master had been fond of him, and he wept aloud, begging the Sheriff to put him out of his misery. So the Sheriff drew his sword, but the master, still crying like a child, exclaimed, Oh! Don't run him through! So the Sheriff got the crowd to separate, so that a current of air could get in. And when the flames burst out fiercely he called to the sufferer to 'swallow the blaze;' which he did, and immediately he sunk dead.'"

There was an appalled silence in the house, and then Finney stepped forward and boomed out, "And these people call themselves Christians?"

"No, no! Shame!" from various parts of the house.

Then Arthur Tappan rose from his seat, trembling, and full of tears. "Dear people," he said, "if you call *yourselves* Christians, then you must call for an end to slavery."

The meeting was over. Emily said, "I can't get over all those people crowding in to watch the burning of a human being—as if it were a show! In a way, they were as guilty as the man who lit the flame!

"They certainly contributed to the poor slave's suffering," Sean said.

"Even *before* that match was lit," Emily said, "he must have suffered...he must have been thinking that soon he would be...*on fire, actually on fire...burning...*that the pain would be awful...awful...and what would he do...what *could* he do...but just die, as soon as possible..."

"Death by fire," said Sean. "It's the stuff of nightmares."

"I know. Ever since you saved me, I've been having dreams like that."

"I'm sorry I brought you to this."

"Don't be. I need to grow up and know these things. I'm grateful you bought me here."

"In spite of your fear of fire? You're a brave girl."

Flames

"The last thing I am is brave. You're the one who's brave."

"Me? Not really. I'm just used to these things. It's amazing what one can get used to."

She took his hand in both of hers and said, "Seanie, is it true that if you breathe enough smoke, you're unconscious by the time you're...on fire?"

"I think so. But let's not talk of it any more. I'd like to introduce you to Arthur Tappan. There's a crowd around him now, but he's well worth waiting in line for."

The couple was now much closer to Tappan; there were only a few people ahead of them in the line. One of them was saying, "Mr. Tappan, I am a Jew, so I don't hold with the theology preached this afternoon. But I *do* admire your efforts to abolish slavery, and I want to contribute to them. Please accept this small donation with my thanks," he said, handing him a sizable stack of bills.

"I thank *you*, sir," said Tappan. "May I know your name?"

"My name is Nehemias Cone," said the man, "and in my tiny way, I've made an effort to lessen the black man's suffering. But my efforts are nothing compared to yours. You have all my good wishes."

Behind Cone, waiting in line, a portly, well-dressed gentleman muttered, "Mr. Cone, you may think better of all your good wishes when you learn the suffering they may cause *you*."

"Sir," said Cone, "I do not understand you."

"Mr. Cone," said the portly man, "you do not *choose* to understand me. Yet my meaning could not be more plain."

"Then let those who choose to understand you do so. As for me, I have a business to run. Your servant, sir." And with that, Nehemias Cone quickly withdrew, giving the portly gentleman his chance with Tappan.

"That man would style himself a businessman," the portly man said to Tappan, "but he's nothing of the kind—he's just a little Jew-tailor with grandiose ambitions."

Said Tappan, "I am privileged, sir, to have a contrary opinion. Is this all you have to say?"

"Will you walk out with me?" the portly man responded, "I have something important to communicate to you."

"Can't you say it here?" said Tappan.

"I'd prefer it to be for your ears only."

"But *I* would prefer there be no secrets. If you don't want anyone else to know what you say, then don't say it to me."

"Very well," said the portly gentleman, "I will say it publicly: Mr. Tappan, we businessmen know that slavery is a great evil, a great wrong; we are not fools. But slavery was consented to by the founding fathers, and provided for in our Constitution. A great portion of the property of the Southerners depends on it and the business of both North and South has become adjusted to it. There are millions upon millions of dollars due from Southerners to the merchants and mechanics of this city alone, the payment of which would be jeopardized by any rupture between the North and the South. We cannot afford, sir, to let you and your associates succeed in your endeavor to overthrow slavery. It is not a matter of principle with us. It is a matter of business necessity. We cannot afford to let you succeed. And I'm telling you now to let you know

Flames

that we mean, sir, to put you abolitionists down—by fair means if we can, by other means if we must."

"Are you threatening me, sir?"

"I'm *informing* you, so you know what you're up against."

"Oh, we know well enough what we're up against. But do you know what *you* are up against, sir? If it were only me, you might have a chance. I myself am a poor sinner, unworthy to lead in this great work. But it is not only me you face. It is not only my colleagues. I am convinced that all the hosts of Heaven are arrayed against you, sir, and that you cannot put abolitionism down." And for the only time that evening, Arthur Tappan raised his voice: "**Slavery is doomed.**"

The portly gentleman shrugged his shoulders and walked away, accompanied by a man dressed in black, a man whose face Emily could not see, but who nonetheless gave her an uncanny shiver of dread when he tossed back his head and let out a sardonic laugh. Involuntarily, she stood closer to Sean. "Who is that man in black?" she whispered, "he gives me the shivers."

"I don't know; I've never seen him before."

Out on the street again, Emily and Sean were walking side by side, but not hand in hand. They were followed—at a discreet distance—by Beatrice.

Emily asked, "when Mr. Tappan said he was a poor sinner, was that false modesty? He seems anything but a sinner."

"From what I can see," said Sean, "Mr. Tappan actually thinks he's unworthy of grace. It doesn't help him to know that much of his business comes from rich Southern plantation owners. But what are we to do? In New York, we're all of us tainted by slavery—everyone who benefits from the shipping industry, or the newspapers—*any industry at all*—is tainted, one way or another. And if Tappan thinks *he's* tainted, God bless him, then so am I, for Heaven's sake, and so is your Da—*especially* your Da—for sure!"

"My father?! What are you talking about?"

"Don't tell me you don't know!"

"Don't know what?"

"Your Da's main stock in trade is lending money to slaveholders. That can't be news to you, surely? They repay the loan by shipping him cotton, which he sells to England for a profit. So he supports slavery by investing in slaveholders."

"How can you say such a thing? My father runs a savings bank—he told me. Once, before I was born, he traded with slaveholders, but never since. He *told* me."

"He tells you everything?"

"Everything important."

"And you tell him everything?"

"I...I try to."

"Have you told him you're seeing me?"

Emily felt a deep hole opening up beneath her. "No," she said. "I haven't."

"It figures. You hold things back from your Da, and he returns the favor."

"What are you implying? I think you're insulting both my father and me!"

"I'm sorry. I just figured that since your father's business is well known in this city, you'd know it, too."

"You're saying my father lied to me?"

"I'm saying he may have thought you too young to know the truth. But you're not a child anymore, I hope." Sean

Flames

took Emily's face in both his hands. "You see, girl, it's not just the South. It's not just your father. It's you and me and everything and everybody. We're all tainted by it. We're *all* dirty."

"I *feel* dirty," she said. "I'm surprised that you'd want to have anything to do with me. Come, Beatrice, we don't want Sean to be any more polluted than he is already! Let's go!"

"Go where?" cried Sean.

"Home! I should never have left it!"

"Oh come on, girl." He tried to embrace her, but she broke away from him.

"Not on the street, Sean! Were you brought up in a barn?"

"Please stay with me a while, Emily."

"So we can rut in some foul sty?

"I'm a pig, am I?!"

"Yes—if you'd have it so! If you want to act like a pig, go ahead! But I'm going home."

"Is that what you do, run home to your Da? You're a spoiled hot-house flower, a baby! No fit woman for a grown man. Go home if you like; I'm done with you!"

She rushed off, holding her cloak close about her to fend off the cold wind. Sean called to her, "come back, Emily! I'm sorry!" But she called out, without turning back, "I'm going home!"

Flames

Sixteen

The man in black

That night, at Thaddeus' house, in the rear parlor, behind the closed pocket partition doors, Emily was helping Beatrice clean up after a dinner for Thaddeus' business associates. Emily was still venting: "A baby, am I? A hot-house flower? No fit woman, am I? Did you hear him, Beatrice?"

"I heard him."

"He thinks I'm still a child—too young to know the truth."

"Is he right?"

"No! At least I hope not."

"How do you find out?"

"Not by kissing on the streets, or...you know...that sort of thing. If that's what he has in mind, let him stay in the barn-yard, where he belongs!"

"You're a very angry young woman."

"He's done with me, he said. And I say fine! I'm done with *him!* You were right, Beatrice: a big, fat no is what I should have told him in the first place. It's over."

"*Perhaps* it is."

"Why only perhaps?"

"A lot can happen. You never know. *I* never knew. When I was sixteen, I was engaged, as I thought, to Robert—as much as slaves like us *could* get engaged. We had a date set, and then two days before the wedding my master ups and says, 'you're leaving. I'm giving you to a Northern banker, to wipe out the debt I owe him.' And that was that. I never saw Robert again. Even if my master had whipped me till my flesh hung in shreds, he wouldn't have hurt me as much as he did the day he sent me away from Robert—to your father, as it happened."

"Yes, I know. You've told me the story."

"It was in Savannah on a Wednesday that I came to your father. He simply didn't know what to do with me! But on Friday, your poor mother died giving birth to you, and then—after he buried her—your father knew what to do. He gave me the charge of caring for you. After I was taken from Robert, caring for you became the most beautiful thing in my life. You were the daughter I always wanted. You were the balm for two broken hearts—your father's and mine."

"And the cause I'm sure for two headaches—my father's and yours."

"I wouldn't worry about it. You've been more than worth it."

"Worth it for you, anyway; Father freed you."

"Not right away. But in 1827, when the law changed, your Father gave me my freedom; he had to. If it weren't for your needing me, I might have left him then and there."

"Tell me, Beatrice, when my mother died, was that when my Father decided to give up his commerce with slaveholders?"

"Is that what he told you?"

Emily nodded.

"Then that's the story."

"Not according to Sean. Sean says that Father's been trading with slaveholders to this day. Is that true?"

"You'll have to ask your father that."

"Why won't you tell me?"

Flames

"The same reason I won't tell your father where you've been going, or who you've been seeing."

"Has he asked you?"

"Many times, honey chile. And just as I've promised you *not* to tell him—I've promised him not to discuss his business with you. That's for him to do."

"I can't believe he would lie to me."

"I know you can't, darlin'."

At that moment, the two women heard the front door bell ring, and they heard Thaddeus calling to Beatrice that she needn't answer it because *he* would, then they heard his speaking sharply: "You again? Don't stand in the doorway like that, we'll all freeze."

Something made Emily put her ear to the partition door so she could hear what was happening on the other side. It was a strange voice she heard, a dark, guttural voice, sounding as if it had risen from the depths of a well: "Let me introduce myself to you at last, Monsieur. I am *Capitaine* Jacques de La Tour, and it is my pleasure to propose business between us."

"I don't care who the hell you are or what your business is," said Thaddeus, "this is my home, not my place of work. If you want to do business with me, make an appointment to see me in my office. Now get out."

"*Pas si vite, pas si vite,* Monsieur: no one is aware I have come to you. And since it is night, they need not know. That is why I like moving in darkness."

The strange visitor, a tall, thin man, clad completely in black, glided into the front parlor, whose many candles, though more than sufficient to illuminate Thaddeus, seemed inadequate to light up this visitor, as if he were cloaked in his own shadow. And when he spoke, his words were as insinuating as his movements: "If you force me to leave too soon, monsieur, I promise you: your whole neighborhood, *vraiment tout le monde* will know my business—and how it relates to yours. I never break a promise; it is not my style."

For a few moments Thaddeus fought the impulse to seize the stranger bodily and throw him out. Finally, having mastered this urge, he said, "Go ahead then, say your piece."

"I am in the slave trade, monsieur; I am Capitaine of a slaving ship, and my expertise is such as could benefit you."

"I fail to see how."

"No? Then allow me to enlighten you. I know precisely how to outfit a slave ship for greatest profit. I know the optimum clearance for the slave deck which will combine the maximum packing with the minimum spoilage."

"Spoilage?"

"Death of cargo. It is always a sad event, monsieur. When we throw their corpses overboard, we are throwing some of our profits overboard, as well. Which means these voyages must be managed with finesse. And I have that finesse, Monsieur; you may trust me on this: I have it! Some of my colleagues allow a mere eighteen inches clearance for the slave deck. How short sighted! *Certainement,* they cram in more cargo, but the death rate is so high and its consequences so costly, that it makes more sense to have clearance that is just a little less cramped. Unlike them, I advocate ten additional inches—twelve at the most. Twenty-eight or thirty inches clearance may seem overly generous, Monsieur, but it makes *good business sense;* I know what I'm doing! With a bit more breathing room, we deliver a healthier product to our customers—they know it—and we can charge far more for it! At the end of the day, our profits are greater! So much so that, at the end of the voyage, we don't have to scrub the ship down to rid it of its filth and pestilence. We can afford simply to burn the ship to the water line, sink it, and buy and outfit a whole new one! Ah monsieur! My family has been in this business for generations, and I myself have been in it for more than ten years: my services are highly valued."

"This is a speech you should be making to slave ship owners, not to me."

"Au contraire, Monsieur, au contraire!" Like a gathering of dark clouds whose shadows hint of a coming storm, de La Tour advanced on Thaddeus. "You are a banker, and I know you will recognize a profitable offer when you see one."

"If it concerns the trafficking in slaves, I am not interested. It is a grim business."

"Certainement," said de La Tour, but the money it makes—don't you love spending it? Everyone does. So we all close our eyes to how it was made, and so should you. Because there is *so much money* to be made with slaves, monsieur! Why merely lend to slave owners and get only a thin slice of their profits—as you are doing now—oh yes: I know exactly what you do! So I know you won't resist the chance to become a slaver yourself, and drink deep at the very teat of profit. It requires no genius to figure it out, *n'est-ce pas?"*

"What do you want?"

"Only a few thousand dollars—say five thousand. That, plus what I have saved, will let me purchase and outfit a small brig—my own ship!—and after the end of its first voyage, you will get many times your investment, and continue to get it with each voyage. I guarantee: it will be the biggest profit you have ever made. You will be my partner—*n'est-ce pas?*—and you will ever thank me, Monsieur."

"I will thank you to leave this house immediately," said Thaddeus with steely reserve. "Give me a while to think it over."

"How much is a while?"

"A few months. This is an important matter, and I'm a busy man. When I have made my decision, I'll send you word, and you can come to *my banking office,* and not my home. Never come here again."

De La Tour had something in his hand: "My card, monsieur." He bowed and left.

And Emily, still standing with her ear against the partition, did not move. Then a smile fluttered on her face, coming and going like a moth before a bright light, and she turned with a little giggle and said: "Isn't it funny? Here I was thinking that none of this slavery business had anything to do with me, that I was a good little girl, high above it all, in a safe place where I could judge all the bloodthirsty people down below. Ha ha!—isn't it hilarious?—I didn't want to know that the house I go to sleep in was built by slaves! That the food I eat, the water I drink, the very clothes on my back—were all bought with their blood, and that I'm drenched in it! Ha ha ha! Isn't it the funniest thing you ever heard? And poor Daddy!" Emily lifted her face to heaven. "Oh God!" she wailed, and she slumped to the floor, sobbing, her face buried in her hands.

For a moment or two, Beatrice simply stood with her arms crossed, looking down on Emily. But then, something broke in Beatrice, too, and she knelt by the girl who was as a daughter to her; she embraced her and stroked her as she said, "oh my dear child, things will seem better in the mornin'."

"No, they won't, they won't—not tomorrow, not the day after that!"

"Look at me, darlin'. I know everything looks hopeless, and life looks like it ain't worth livin'. I know what that's like. But I also know that some mornin' or other, the sun will come up like glory, blazing with the hope it brings. That's what happened to me. It will happen to you too, honey chile, trust me." And she gathered Emily into her arms, where she sobbed uncontrollably.

Flames

Seventeen
The book isn't finished on any of us.

A few days later, with the sun very low in the sky, and with the late afternoon light warming the dining room, Thaddeus and Emily sat at the supper table, which was amply supplied with food. Thaddeus' plate was empty, for he had eaten everything on it, but Emily's, in contrast, was still laden with pot roast, carrots, green beans, and mashed potatoes. "You've scarcely touched your plate, Emily," he said; "you've been pecking at it like a bird. What's the matter?"

"Nothing, really, Father. I'm just not hungry."

"I had Cook make all your favorites. You used to love mashed potatoes and gravy; is there something wrong with it? It tasted fine to me."

"I'm sure it *is* fine—I'm just not hungry, that's all. May I be excused, please?"

At this point Beatrice came in. "We're having ice cream for dessert," she said, *"vanilla* ice cream—I made it just for you. Wouldn't you like a little?"

"I'm sorry, Beatrice." Emily rose. "I'd like to lie down, Father, if you don't mind."

He rose, and went to her. "You go ahead, baby; lie down if you like. Catch up on sleep. Maybe that's what you need. When you wake up, I hope you'll feel better." He gave her a kiss.

"Thanks, Father." Emily went to her room.

"She's barely eaten a thing in three days," said Beatrice. "This can't go on."

"You're right," Thaddeus said. "Shall we send for a doctor?"

"There's not much a doctor can do, in my opinion."

"Good heavens—you don't mean—"

"Nothing like that," Beatrice interrupted. "She's not mortally ill, so far as I know."

"What *do* you know?"

"She's lost her appetite because she's deeply unhappy."

"About what?"

"Ask her."

"I have, but she doesn't want to talk about it. I'm asking what *you* know."

"I can't talk about that."

"You can't talk?! What the hell is this? You work for me, for Christ's sake!"

Beatrice's smile had more than a trace of irony. "But I'm no longer your slave," she said, "if that's what you mean. Just as you've asked me not to discuss your business with Emily, your daughter has asked me not to discuss with you *her* business."

"Whatever she does is my business."

"That's not how she sees it. She relies on me to keep her confidences, just as you rely on me to keep yours."

The look Thaddeus gave Beatrice was smoking with fury. "I could fire you on the spot."

"Yes you could, but I doubt you're that stupid. I've been a mother to Emily all her life, I've kept her on an even keel, taught her; I've comforted her when she needed it. Right now she needs me more than ever. I know you too well, Mr. Bender. You're not going to wound her like that, and you know it."

Flames

For a moment, Thaddeus looked as if he actually might strike her. But then, the stuffing seemed to go out of him, and he slowly sat down. "May I ask, at least, whether Emily's in trouble?"

"She's not—at least not in the way you may be thinking. She's done nothing wrong. But unless we do something, she may get seriously ill. In that way, she *is* in trouble, and we'd better act fast."

"What can we do?"

"I've made an outline of what we could try." Beatrice produced a page of foolscap, covered with handwriting, and gave it to Thaddeus. He scanned it.

"Interesting," he said. And not without expense."

"No daughter is without expense," replied Beatrice. "But Emily's worth it."

"Absolutely," he said. "But will all this work?"

"It's worth a try. But whatever you do, Mr. Bender, don't say a word to Emily about this conversation, much less the plan. If we do it right, Emily should think it's her own idea."

Thaddeus sighed in relief. "Thank you, Beatrice."

"You're welcome."

Thaddeus looked away. There was a moment of silence which Beatrice was careful not to violate. Finally Thaddeus said, "It was foolish of me to pull the Master/Employer business on you. You don't deserve it."

"You're too hard on yourself. You've been worried sick about Emily—just as I've been."

"When I look at her, I see her mother."

"When she looks at you, Mr. Bender, she sees the father she has idolized."

"It's been too great a burden. I can't live up to it. Compared to what she expects of me, I'm venal and materialistic."

"I won't fight you there, Thaddeus Bender."

"Now that you know I'm not likely to fire you any time soon, you dare address me by my first name—as if you were my equal?"

"I *am* your equal, Mr. Bender—not in riches or power, certainly—but I am a human being, just like you. And at the end, my lot will be six feet of earth—no more and no less than yours."

"That's true enough."

"And while you're hearing the truth, I might as well tell you that even though you freed me in 1827, I still saw you as the slave owner's banker, and I considered leaving you then and there. I didn't, because I loved Emily too much, and because I thought no man so devoted to his daughter can be *all bad*."

"Right now I'm grateful for any compliment, even a back handed one like that."

"Let's see how things work out. God willing, the book isn't finished on *any* of us."

Mid morning, two days later, Emily looked for Beatrice and found her in the kitchen, on the first floor, some four feet below street level. There was a great kettle of stew cooking on the stove, and the kitchen was redolent with food preparation, on which Cook and Beatrice were collaborating.

"Oh!" cried Emily, "you seem to be preparing a feast!"

"Would you like some?" Beatrice said. "There's plenty to go around."

"I'm not really hungry. But what's the occasion?"

Flames

"Late this afternoon, I'm having this sent over to Joe Simon's family. They live near Five Points."

"Who's Joe Simon?"

"Who *was* Joe Simon? He was a black man, made his living as a carter on the docks. A gang of white dock workers cut him to pieces—because they felt like it—no other reason. He left a wife with a young daughter, and a newborn son."

"Horrible."

"Yes. I found out about her the other day. She's been taking in washing and sewing—making barely enough to keep her family fed. She's very bitter. She knows that her husband was killed only because of the color of his skin, and she has similar prejudices against white people."

"I understand. But why are you going to all the trouble of having this big supper carted down to Five Points? The Simon family could come here."

"Won't the neighbors fuss?" asked Beatrice.

"Let them; this is our house. Besides, the Simons can come in by the servant's entrance—right here. So long as we're clean and quiet, the neighbors should have nothing to complain about."

"What about your father?"

"Leave him to me; he won't be a problem. You just go down to Five Points right now and tell Mrs. Simon they're invited here. It makes no difference what they wear or how they look. We're not like those dock workers."

Beatrice shared a covert glance with Cook, and then proceeded: "Emily, I can't go right now; Cook needs me to help her."

"No, you can go ahead; I'll take your place and won't mind doing it—this stew smells delicious."

"Well, why not taste it to make *sure* it is?"

"Really? I suppose tasting a little bit wouldn't hurt..."

Beatrice handed her a wooden spoon full of stew. "Blow on this first, honey, it's hot..."

Emily tried some. "Oh God, that's good," she said, "I had forgotten how hungry I am! Could you spare a little more?"

Cook spoke up in her curious baritone: "We have enough here to feed *three* families!"

Beatrice ladled some stew into a small bowl. "Have some of this, darlin', a little at a time; don't wolf it down. I'm off to the Simons. I'll tell them to be here by three-thirty?"

"That'll give us plenty of time," Cook intoned deeply. "Right, Miss Emily?"

But Emily was so busy eating the stew that she didn't see the cook's sly wink at Beatrice, nor did she notice Beatrice's knowing smile.

The next day, Beatrice was in Thaddeus' home office. "I assume it must have gone well," he told her, "Emily was ravenous at breakfast—downed a stack and a half of pancakes!"

"Yes, it went very well," said Beatrice. "While I was out, Emily chopped and diced as if she were born to it. She even made a few suggestions to Cook, who took them all!"

"Amazing. You must have primed Cook ahead of time."

"I did lay down the law a bit—so Cook was as gentle as a lamb—quite out of character. But Emily was so eager to help, she didn't notice a thing. And she insisted on waiting on the Simons herself. The elder child—the little girl—was a bit sullen. Probably has picked up her mother's attitude. But Mrs. Simon, to her credit, insisted that the little girl thank Emily politely. And she assured us that the little boy thanked us, too—though all he could actually say was *Mama!* When the whole thing was over, Emily presented the little girl with a drawing she had once made—you know the one with flowers in a bowl?"

"Like the one I have in my office? You're telling me she *gave* it to her?"

"That's right. But don't worry; there's more where that came from."

"Where's Emily now? "

"In the kitchen with Cook, planning menus. Emily wants to do this once a week. And she wants to add one more family to the guest list. The widow of an Irish laborer—Gallagher, I think her name is. Husband got hit with a ton of bricks. Left her with two kids. Emily said she brought food and blankets to them once, but heaven knows how that family's surviving; they've got no visible means of support. Maybe the Church is helping."

"A black family and a white family—in the same room, eating?"

"That's the plan. Once a week."

"Once a week?! For how long?"

"Heaven only knows; Emily hasn't told me yet."

"Unbelievable!"

"We knew it was going to be expensive."

"The expense is the least of it. It's just that...well...to use my home as a...charity house?!"

"Mr. Bender, for Emily to have an appetite, her hands need people to help. The more the better. You'll see: she'll feel even better next week."

Next week in the Benders' kitchen, the widow Simon and her children were being served their first course when there was a knock on the door. Emily went to open it and found the widow Gallagher and *her* family. Emily and Mrs. Gallagher exchanged cordial greetings and an embrace. "So good to see you again, Mrs. Gallagher," cried Emily, "come on in—you're all welcome!" The Gallaghers entered, but when they and the Simons saw each other, both families froze as if the temperature had suddenly dropped 50 degrees. Mrs. Simon stood up rigid, and the little girl, open mouthed, dropped her steel spoon onto her plate, making an ear-stabbing clatter.

"Miss Emily," Mrs. Simon said, "you never said *they* were coming."

"I wanted it to be a surprise," Emily said brightly. "It sounded like a good idea—you and Mrs. Gallagher have a lot in common."

"I and that white woman have a lot in common?"

A painful silence.

"Well, you both lost your husbands at about the same time. Each of you has two kids to support—and not much money to do it with. I'd say you have a lot to talk about."

Another silence. Then the widow Simon spoke: "Miss Emily, you mean well. And you have a big heart; I'm grateful for it. But please don't meddle in what you don't understand. If I and that white woman have a lot to talk about, rearin' a family is the least of it, so far as I'm concerned. If we have to talk, let's talk about how in this city, a man can be butchered just because he's black! Let's talk about how, for Mrs. Whitey here, I'm nothin' but a nigger! And how, for this nigger, *there must be justice!* The widow Simon was almost screaming, and her baby had started to cry. Mrs. Simon picked up the infant,

Flames

and for a few moments, soothed him: "There, there, little one. You weren't expecting this, and neither was I."

When the baby's crying had subsided, Mrs. Gallagher spoke very quietly: "Mrs. Simon: my name is Mrs. Gallagher, not Mrs. Whitey. And the last thing I want is to upset you, or anyone else. And since you apparently set great store on having got here first, I'll take my leave. Miss Emily, please forgive me."

She turned to go, but Beatrice said loudly, "You've done nothing wrong, Mrs. Gallagher."

"Miss Beatrice is right," Emily said. "In addition, we went to a lot of trouble and expense making a dinner for you and your family. Don't thank me—just eat. That goes for you, too, Mrs. Simon. You don't have to talk to each other. All you have to do is just *eat the food.* Your children are hungry. You owe it to them. So please, for the love of Jesus, sit down and eat what's been prepared for you."

Neither family moved.

"Will you please sit down," said Emily, *"please?"* She ladled a bowl full of stew and held it out. *"Please?"*

At length, Mrs. Gallagher's little boy sat down. Emily quickly put the bowl of stew in front of him, and quietly said, "you can start eating, Matt, it's all right." The boy fell to, which encouraged Mrs. Simon's daughter to sit down as well; she was rewarded with her own bowl of stew, and she started eating.

"The children know best," said Mrs. Gallagher, who sat down with her baby, leaving Mrs. Simon, holding her infant son, standing alone. Finally Mrs. Simon sat down, smarting with humiliation.

When all were finally eating, Emily wished them all a good appetite, informed them that Beatrice and she were going upstairs for a brief while, that Cook would serve them, and that they would return before supper was over.

Upstairs, in the front parlor, Beatrice said, "I hope I wasn't speaking out of turn down there."

"No no, Beatrice; I was tongue-tied. If you hadn't spoken up, I might have let Mrs. Gallagher leave. But you made me realize that this project is one I really should take charge of. Do you mind?"

"Not a bit, honey chile. You're the one to run this thing. I've thought so from the beginning."

"But all that hatred and distrust—appalling! When Mrs. Simon started screaming, I was amazed! Weren't you?"

"Actually no, dear. I've been through it too many times."

"Of course you have. That was a stupid thing for me to say."

"Not stupid, dear—just inexperienced. But you'll learn fast."

"I hope so. I really hope I can get those two families to be nice to each other."

"I hope you can, too, child. But don't be too disappointed if you fail at first. These hatreds take years to build up, and it'll take more than a good meal to heal them. Some day there will be peace between the races, though we ourselves may never see it. Your children may not, nor their children. Even their great-grandchildren may not see it. But someday it will happen. It has to. Meanwhile, we must do what we can, and have faith."

Flames

Back in the kitchen, the supper was over, and Mrs. Gallagher was rising from the table. "That was so good," she told Cook, "I can't thank you enough. I only wish Miss Emily and Miss Beatrice were down here, so I could thank them as well."

At this moment, Emily and Beatrice appeared, and Emily said, "it's we who thank *you,* Mrs. Gallagher, for giving us the chance to help. But where is Mrs. Simon?"

"She left early," said Mrs. Gallagher. "Her daughter looked like she could do with a little more, but out they went."

"Too bad," said Emily, "I'd like to have thanked her as well. Does she know she is welcome next week, at the same time?"

"I told her, Miss Emily," Cook growled, "but I don't know if she'll come or not."

"If she finds another source of food," said Beatrice, "she may not come. Otherwise, she may find the need to live is greater than the need to get even. I think we'll see her."

"I'm so grateful that you've invited us, Miss Emily," said Mrs. Gallagher. "We'll be here with bells on."

"Wonderful. But before you leave, may I ask if you've seen Sean—Mr. Dougherty? Or heard word of him?"

"I haven't seen him, Miss Emily, but I *have* heard word of him. My cousin Timothy serves in his fire company and sees him all the time."

"Is he well?" said Emily, trying not to sound too anxious.

"Well enough, Tim said—although now, in the firefighting, he's given to taking more chances than he used to. Still, he seems to be having fun, for all that. Tim saw him at St.

Patrick's social evening, squiring not just one but two young ladies, and dancing hard enough to wear out his shoes."

"Oh!" cried Emily, feeling struck in the chest. "Well, he's an active young man, and you cannot expect men like that to...to sit still." A little shaky, she leaned forward to steady herself on the kitchen table, briefly closing her eyes. Then she opened them and turned to the mason's widow. "I mustn't keep you, Mrs. Gallagher. Do come to us next week."

"Thank you, Miss Emily," said Mrs. Gallagher, dropping a deep curtsey, then leaving.

Emily sank slowly down upon the rough-hewn bench that her guests had used. She covered her face with her hands.

Beatrice went to her and placed a hand on her shoulder. "Are you all right, honey?"

"Sure I am—just a little weak in the knees, is all. I'll be fine in a moment."

"I was going to ask you to keep me company tomorrow in the market place—we're going to need a lot more food than usual."

"Forgive me Beatrice, but I don't think I'll feel up to it. My place is home—right here, helping you and Cook prepare things. Is that all right? I just don't want to be seen right now."

"And so her answer was, 'I don't feel up to it—I don't want to be seen right now,'" said Beatrice to Thaddeus in his home office. "I'm afraid it's going to be a while before we can get her back to her old self."

"I understand," said Thaddeus. "But at least she's eating again. And I have you to thank for that."

"Thank *the Lord* for that, Thaddeus."

Flames

If the Buddha in the tavern was trying to get Sean to cease caring about inevitable loss, it failed more dismally than before. For once again the young fireman was at his customary dark table, this time a half empty pint of whisky in front of him. He poured a slug from it into a glass, drank it, and closed his eyes. They opened quickly, however, when he heard: "Sean, Sean my boy, how lucky my Freedom Night coincides with yours, how lucky!" It was Egmont, who with theatrical panache, had just entered the tavern. He strode up to Sean and said, "My heavens, lad, you look much the worse for wear, ha, ha! What's happened?"

"She's gone, that's what's happened."

"Why?"

"Maybe she got tired of slumming? No, she's not like that. The real reason is I drove her away. I kept insisting on how tainted we all are by the slave business—especially her father, whom she looks up to. She feels awful, and it's *my fault;* that's what's killing me! Satisfied? Now get the hell out of here."

"I am desolate, my boy. What a way to talk to a friend!"

"You're my friend, are you?"

"Well, I was going to suggest you visit a waitress upstairs at my expense, though in your condition, I'm not sure you'd be able to...er...hold up your end of things—not sure at all."

"Please stop bothering me with that...that *shit.* Who do you work for—a whore master?"

"A whore master? *No, no,* no! I work for a banker."

"A banker, is it? They're almost as bad."

At this point, Egmont dropped his manic façade, and said, quite seriously, "Take my word for it, Sean: they're worse."

Flames

Eighteen

Consequences

Emily tried to keep busy: she made it a rule to be up an hour before dawn, and by 7AM had fixed breakfast for herself, bathed, dressed, and had neatened her room. Then she would check the larder and would note on a shopping list any incipient shortages. Having seen to that, she'd make sure that the front and back parlors were tidied and dusted. On Thursday, she would confer with Cook about the menu for Friday's hosting of the Gallaghers and Simons, then she'd refine the shopping list and send Cook and Beatrice off to market. Early the next morning, she'd join them in the kitchen to help prepare that supper, the guests of which she'd personally serve later that day.

But most weekdays, once she had seen to the house's good order, she'd retire to her own room and recline on a chaise longue, to read such fare as Jane Austen's *Pride and Prejudice,* and Godwin's *Cloudesley.* Next to the chaise longue was a small table piled high with such books, provided by Thaddeus at her request. Sitting uncomfortably among these novels—like a stranger in a strange land—was Adam Smith's *The Wealth of Nations,* which she had made a point of requesting, but could not bring herself to read.

Except for her Sunday devotions at the Methodist church, she rarely ventured outside, preferring the seclusion of her home. *At least I am not moping around,* she would think. *No: I am of service to people—at least to the Gallaghers and the Simons. And I am occupied by reading, which—if it's not really* improving *my mind, at least, hopefully, it's keeping it from crumbling. Nothing is crumbling! So nobody can accuse me of being crushed by this business with Sean. Oh no—my life is in good order.*

After one such soothing train of thought, on a Tuesday evening after supper, Beatrice appeared with news that tested Emily's optimism: "Emily, you have a visitor."

"Really? Is there a visiting card?"

"I doubt he has one."

"He...?"

"Sean."

"Sean!" For weeks, Emily had kept telling herself that she was *over* that man. So why was her heart pounding?

"Shall I let him in?"

"Can't we tell him that I'm not at home?"

"Emily, **we** cannot tell him anything. If you are not at home to him, you are going to have to send that message yourself. And I should tell you: he sees the lamp glowing in this room, so he guesses you're home—he said so."

"I don't think I'm up to seeing him."

"Then you have two choices: tell him you don't want to see him, or do see him—and find out if you're up to it. What'll it be?"

Emily sighed. "I'll see him."

"In your bedroom?" Beatrice asked.

"No, no, of course not. Let me go down to the front parlor. Once I'm there, you can let him in."

Beatrice nodded and headed for the stairs; Emily took a hair brush and gave her hair three swift strokes. Then she quickly went down the stairs to the front parlor, only to discover Sean standing there—Beatrice had already let him in.

Flames

He looks pale...drawn, she thought. *I wonder if I look that way to* him*?*

"Hello Sean," she said.

"Hello; I'm glad to see you."

"Will you sit down?"

"Thank you." Sean sat on the sofa nearest to him; Emily chose the other sofa, on the opposite wall. "This is ridiculous," Sean said. "There must be fifteen feet between us. May I move a chair? So we won't have to sit so far apart?"

"If you like."

So Sean moved a side chair closer to Emily's sofa, then sat on it. "Thank you," he said.

"You're welcome."

"This is so much better, isn't it?" he said, "being closer and all?" She said nothing. "This is a very nice room," he said, "in fact the whole house seems very nice."

"Is that what you've come to tell me," she said, "that my house seems nice?" She saw the stricken look on Sean's face, and instantly regretted her words. "Sorry."

"Don't be," he said, "and I didn't come to talk about your house. I wanted to tell you how sorry I was for having said...what I did. There was no excuse for hurting your feelings that way."

"Would there have been a better way to hurt my feelings?"

"No good way at all. I shouldn't have hurt them, period."

"Perhaps you are worrying too much about it. As you can see, *this* 'hothouse flower' has survived quite nicely."

"I am so sorry I called you that."

"Sorry? Don't waste your time. As you've said, I'm a daddy's girl, and now that I've run home to Daddy, I feel perfectly safe, and ready to forget the whole thing."

"The whole thing?"

"The things you said. The things *I* said. Everything. It never happened."

"You mean, the words we had at Finney's revival meeting?"

"Not only those," said Emily, feeling a gnawing at her insides, a widening hole within her, "I mean *everything*: the fire engine race, the visit to the firehouse, the fire ruins, Tappan's Warehouse—**everything**. It never happened. None of it." Emily looked away, so that Sean would not see the tears welling in her eyes.

There was a painful silence. Then Sean spoke very quietly: "And thus, with one stroke, you would wipe away everything we shared, everything we *were* to each other?"

"What were we? Casual pals—good for a walk in the slums. What did we share? One kiss. That was nice, very nice to be sure, but nothing to lose sleep over." *I won't let him know how much sleep* I've *lost over it!* I'll tell you what you were for me: a contact with a world felt I should know more about. And what was I for you? A contact with a world *it was to your advantage* to get closer to." *Not bad for Daddy's little girl! Not bad for a hot-house flower!*

"You're saying my interest in you has been materialistic?!"

"Well hasn't it been? After coming here, virtually your first words were what a nice room this was, and what a nice house I had!" By this time, Emily was crying, and she didn't care who saw it. All she could hear was her father's voice, say-ing, *No one should do that. Not to us. There are consequences.*

"Oh, my darlin' girl..." said Sean, rising to go to her.

"I'm *not* your darlin' girl!" she said, also rising. "I'll nev-er be *anybody's* darlin' girl!"

"You'll always be *my* darlin' girl, whether you like or not!" And his arms were around her and he was kissing her hair, her brow, her cheek...and she stood there passively, let-ting him.

"Seanie, Seanie," she said finally, "please do me a favor, and leave me...it can never work between us..." And her fa-ther's voice inside her was saying, *there are consequences...!*

"Because of the money thing? I don't *care* about the money!"

If you love me, Seanie, the best thing you can do for me is leave—right now."

"Why are you acting this way, Emily? I've never seen you like this. Just explain what's going on, and I'll leave."

In a strangled voice, Emily said—for the first time out loud—"There are consequences."

Sean Dougherty, after a final disbelieving look at her, turned on his heel, walked out the door, and closed it quietly behind him.

"There are consequences!" she cried to the closed door, "and I hate them! I hate them!" And the face of Emily Bend-er—now that there was nobody to see it—crumbled.

After that, Emily's world gave way to a gray sameness. What time was it? What *day* was it? She wasn't sure, nor did she care, particularly. Her duty, as she saw it, was merely to go through the motions, which day after day, she did—

meticulously. She was conscious that her house had become a mausoleum in which she had buried herself alive, but she thought that appropriate. She threw out the romances that her father had brought her, and found herself dressing in black. She was aware that other people her age were flirting and courting, but that was nothing to her. If they wanted to waste their time on such vanity, let them. And with thoughts like these, Emily felt the hours, days, and weeks meld into a gray blur.

Flames

Nineteen
Some pleasant conversation

It was 2:30, Saturday afternoon, and Egmont was in front of Cone's Custom Clothing. The door was closed; he tried it, but it seemed barred shut. He knocked, and when no one seemed to be coming, he turned away, only to hear the door being unbarred. He turned to see the door open, revealing Rachel. "Oh, Mr. Egmont," she said.

"Just Egmont. Call me Egmont."

"Well sir...Egmont...we're closed today. It's Shabbos. We do no work today."

"Forgive me," said Egmont, "I should have remembered. But may I ask, if it's your Sabbath, what are you doing in the store?"

"It's our home; we live upstairs."

At that moment, they heard the voice of Nehemias, who was coming down the stairs: "Rachel, who's at the door?"

"Father, this is Egmont, a customer."

"Didn't you tell him it's Shabbos?"

"She did, sir," said Egmont, thinking quickly, "but my real reason for coming is to see if I could go for a walk with your daughter—with your permission, of course."

Both Rachel and her father looked equally astonished. Nehemias recovered first. "Egmont?" he said, "your name is Egmont?"

"It is, sir."

"What kind of name is that?"

"It's what people call me. But my real name is Ezekiel."

"Ah, *Ezekiel!*" cried Nehemias. "You mean, *Yechezqel? As in God strengthens?*"

"Exactly, sir."

"Where would you go, *Yechezqel?*"

"Not far, sir. Perhaps around the block, if your daughter is willing."

Nehemias turned toward his daughter. "You've been working so hard, Rachel. Do you think a little Shabbos sunshine would do you good?"

Rachel did not have to think fast, for she had already made up her mind.

"Certainly, if you think so, father. I'd be glad for the walk."

Egmont offered his arm, and off they went. As soon as Nehemias had gone inside, Egmont turned to her and said, "I am here under false pretences. I let your father think I am Jewish, but I'm not. I'm Lutheran; Egmont is my real name; and my parents are back in Germany, where I come from."

As if by mutual consent, they stopped walking. She looked at him. "If my father had known all that, he would never have allowed this walk," she said. "He doesn't believe in spending time when not much can come of it."

"I understand," Egmont said, "Which is why I did not disabuse him. And the situation is even less promising than I've made out. For even if I were Jewish, I'd have scant prospects, since Thaddeus Bender pays me scarcely enough to keep me in kippers, let alone support a family."

"Of course," said Rachel, "you could always ask for a raise."

"Also I could convert to Judaism, though my boss isn't likely to fall in love with that idea, either. Which means that as

Flames

things stand, you're wasting your time with me. All I can offer you is some pleasant conversation."

"Then, Mr. Egmont, you had better make some."

"I'll tell you this: before seeing you, I thought I had trained myself to resist feminine charm. But now I realize I'm abjectly susceptible to it."

She laughed. "That's a very good start. What girl wouldn't want to hear more of the same? Still I ought to tell you that if a man with likelier prospects came around, I'd be bound to spend my time with *him.*"

"No doubt," he said. "And I have to say I'm surprised that promising young men have not already come around."

"Oh they have, they have. But I haven't cared for any of them. And father is too good a man to force on me anyone I don't care for."

"I'm grateful for that. Still, I'm aware that a young man far likelier than I may come along any minute."

"Which means," she said, "that we had better enjoy each other's company while we can."

He smiled at her. "My thought precisely," he said.

Flames

Twenty
I'm well rid of you

Almost a year later—it was late autumn in 1835 when Thaddeus heard on the door of his home office a knock much firmer than he had heard in a while, and a stronger voice from Emily than he had heard recently: "Can I come in, Daddy?"

"Of course! Come right on in," he said, preparing to rise to open the door for her. But she opened it before he had a chance to get up.

"No need to get up, Daddy," she said, "here I am!" And she entered and bestowed a kiss on her father.

"I'm glad to see you in such fine fettle," he said. "What can I do for you?"

"You can buy me a new dress, if you wouldn't mind."

"Mind? I'd love it! How many dresses would you like?"

"Just one, Daddy—at least for now."

"Is there one you saw in a store somewhere, that I could get you?"

"No, not really. Just get whatever you can find that's stylish and fun."

"Whatever *I* can find? Emily, I'm a banker, not a connoisseur of fashion. Why don't you go out and choose one yourself?"

"I'm not quite ready to go out, Daddy. But with a new dress, I might have the courage to be seen."

"Hm. I have the perfect solution."

"I knew you would, Daddy!"

"I've been getting my shirts and other things made at that Jew-Tailor's shop—Cone's. The work was done by his daughter, actually. I could send for her; she could come here, and you could tell her what you want; she'd make it at the shop and fit you here. How does that sound?"

"It sounds wonderful! I'm so relieved!"

"Because you're not quite ready to go out, eh? Hm. Yet you're *almost* ready? What's happened?"

"I suddenly had a very profound insight, Father."

"And that is…"

"Why should everyone else have all the fun? I deserve some, too!"

"It took you long enough to figure that out!"

"What can I tell you, Daddy? I'm a slow learner."

Not long thereafter, Rachel was measuring Emily in the rear parlor, and with an endless supply of pins, was draping and fitting to her large swaths of muslin.

"And the sleeves will have light blue stripes?" Emily asked.

"Yes, Miss Emily," Rachel said.

"And dark blue piping?"

"The entire dress will have dark blue piping—just as you've ordered, Miss Emily."

"I can hardly wait!"

"I'll make it as fast as I can, but please understand that there are many people ahead of you. Thanks be to God, business is not only good, it's overwhelming. I'm fitting you in as a special favor to your father."

"You don't have to hurry, Rachel. When I get the dress, I'll feel pressure from my father to go out and wear it. I'm in no rush for that."

Flames

There was a silence while Rachel continued to work, and then Emily said, "Rachel, do you have a beau?"

"I don't know," Rachel replied.

"I don't understand."

"Neither do I, really. There *is* a young man whom I like very much—he's witty, intelligent and fun, and he's respectful of me—treats me like a queen. He's led my father to believe that he's Jewish, but he's confided to me that he isn't—that he's really Lutheran."

"Interesting!"

"It gets more interesting—I've observed him quite carefully, and occasionally he lets slip some Yiddish expression or other..."

"Yiddish?"

"Jewish language. Not only does he say a few things in Yiddish, but he understands some of the Hebrew characters on our posters. He always has a plausible explanation for all this, but...well...I don't know how to say it, but...when you're with another Jew, there are some things that you don't have to explain—and it has nothing to do with religion. I can't really tell you why, but I'm convinced that he really *is* Jewish, but doesn't want anyone to know."

"I wonder why not?"

"If non-Jews don't know you're Jewish, often they'll treat you better. And Egmont..."

"Egmont?"

"My beau. As I was going to say, Egmont's afraid even to ask his boss for a raise, so he's unlikely to tell him he's a Jew. And yet he might just as well—his boss pays him a paltry salary for all the work he does—barely a living wage for one person, let alone a family—he could scarcely treat him worse."

145

"His boss sounds like a tough character. Who is he?"

"Your father, Miss Emily."

"What?!"

"Egmont works in your father's bank."

"Shall I...shall I speak to my father?"

"Please don't. That would be going behind Egmont's back, and he would never forgive me. But I've got to do *something.* If Egmont doesn't propose soon, my father will pressure me to consider other suitors—there are plenty of them. But I want only Egmont, and he seems unable to move. I don't know what to do."

Emily considered it briefly, then said, "It's funny how easy it is to advise others on their love lives, when you can't figure out your own."

"It's easy to advise me?"

"Very. Just tell Egmont that you need your relationship to move forward to the next stage—engagement. Tell him you feel sure he's Jewish, but if he doesn't propose, you will tell your father what he told you—that he's Lutheran. And that will effectively end it between you."

"But what if he doesn't propose?"

"Then you're well rid of him."

"It would break my heart."

"Better for him to break it now, when you're still young and pretty enough to attract someone else."

"You're right, Miss Emily—but oh, you're tough too, just like your father."

"That has occurred to me."

"You would tell your father that?" said Egmont to Rachel during their customary Shabbos walk. "That would end everything between us. He would never allow us to see each other."

"It wouldn't have to end if we became engaged," Rachel said.

"With my pitiful income, I dare not propose to you, Rachel."

"Ask Mr. Bender for a raise. Tell him why."

"I'm afraid of that."

"Shall I tell you what you're afraid of?" she cried, eyes flashing.

"Go ahead," said Egmont, his eyes downcast.

"You're afraid to *marry me*," she said, "because then the world would know that you're Jewish, and for some reason that scares you. And apparently my poor self isn't enough to persuade you. Emily Bender was right: I'm well rid of you."

Flames

Twenty-One
My name is Emily

It was Sunday afternoon, and Emily was standing at the front door of Mr. and Mrs. Edward Bass's home. Emily hoped that Mrs. Bass—the former Sarah Cunningham, Emily's best friend at Mrs. Okill's school—would like her new dress, just finished by Rachel Cone. The door opened to reveal not Mrs. Bass, but her maid. Emily presented her visiting card. "Wait just a moment, miss," said the maid, who disappeared briefly, then returned to say: "Mrs. Bass is in the parlor. This way please." Emily was ushered into Sarah Bass's parlor.

Sarah rose to greet her: "Emily Bender—how lovely to see you again; it's been—well, how long *has* it been—almost *a full year* since we've seen you? Far too long! You seemed to have disappeared—or worse, gone to Philadelphia? Are you quite well? You look so pale. Please do sit down. We have, as my husband likes to say, tea and cakes at the ready. I wonder if Edward knows you are here, because if he did he would surely come down to greet you. He's very proper."

"Yes, of course," said Emily.

The tea and cakes promptly appeared, neatly arranged on little silver plates.

"Oh, look—the goodies," exclaimed Sarah. "Have as much as you want; we like to prepare enough for whatever visitors may come Sunday afternoons, and what with today's endless round, I fear I've been snacking far too much and gaining too much weight. But Edward said it's perfectly proper for a wife to gain a little weight, and indeed it's healthful.

149

And Edward knows about such things, so I always take his advice. Oh, but look, he's coming, I knew he would."

Edward Bass appeared, bowed formally to Emily and said, "Charmed to make your acquaintance, Miss. I don't believe I've had the pleasure...?"

"Oh, but Edward," said Sarah. Bass, "this is Emily Bender, my old school friend. She was kind enough to attend our wedding, don't you remember?"

"Oh, of course, Miss Bender, you're the daughter of the dry goods importer?"

"No no, dear," said Mrs. Bass, "don't you remember, she's the daughter of Thaddeus Bender, the cotton factor."

"Of course, of course," said her husband, "a very important man in this city, how could I have forgotten? Blame it on the hardware—I'm a hardware man—always thinking of it...in fact, gotta get back to it."

He started to leave, but his wife said, "But dearest, today is Sunday, and Miss Bender is paying us a social call."

"Much obliged to you, Miss Bender, but if I talked with every visitor who came, I'd get nothing done. And in today's world, success comes to the man who works not only on work days, but *every* day. That's *my* job. But talking with visitors— that's my wife's job. And so I leave you with her; you're in good hands, Miss Bender." And he departed quickly.

"Oh, isn't he so *competent,* Emily? Edward knows everything."

"I'm sure he does."

"I leave everything to him."

"You're very lucky."

"But now," said Sarah, "what have you been doing all this time, wherever it was you were doing it?"

Flames

What am I going to say to her? "Well, I've been...that is, I've become interested in...learning a little about...some of the abolition societies that are springing up everywhere."

"Oh!" cried Sarah Bass, "and aren't they such a nuisance? Making trouble, causing riots, shaking the very foundations of our democracy!"

"Do you really think that?"

"Well that's what Edward thinks; he's given it a lot of thought, and I trust him on these things. Politics are better left to the men, don't you think? That's their sphere. They're supposed to know about that sort of thing, and I know Edward does. He knows everything."

It was a few days later, a weekday, around 2 in the afternoon, that Emily, by herself, went into the New York Public Gardens, whose headwaiter said it was nice to see her after so long an absence. "Where have you been?" he asked.

"Nowhere special." She ordered vanilla ice cream, and when the waiter brought it, he asked where was that handsome young Sean who used to bring her there—was he well? Emily said that she supposed so, but that in truth, she hadn't seen him for a while. "Oh," said the waiter, "sorry," and he placed the dish of ice cream in front of the young woman, and quickly retreated. Emily took a scant spoonful, then placed the spoon down on the dish, and left the rest uneaten.

She heard a dark, quietly insinuating voice: "Mam'selle, you should eat that ice cream before it melts. It would be a shame to let it spoil." She lifted her eyes to see oozing up from his table the voice's owner, a coarse looking, thin man, some twenty years her senior, and dressed completely in black. "Likewise," he said, "it would be a shame to let so pretty a girl

151

as you dine all by herself. *N'est-ce pas?* I cannot allow this. It is not my style." He sauntered over to her.

"Oh God," she quavered, thinking she had heard his voice before.

He laughed: "Perhaps you recognize me? Then you won't mind if I keep you company."

She looked as if she was about to bolt. "Please don't bother," she managed, "I'm all right."

But the man was not deterred. "Ah, but I insist," he said, and was about to sit down when a stranger—a young man in a Lieutenant's uniform—appeared as if out of nowhere. It was Benjamin Livingston.

"You've heard the lady," he told the offensive one, "so do us all a favor and leave. Now." The intruder was about to offer violence when Benjamin produced a pistol. "Leave this instant," he said quietly, "or you're a dead man. And it will be my pleasure."

The intruder backed away. "You have tried to humiliate Jacques de La Tour," he said. "That takes courage. You will need it when we meet again, for then the pleasure will be all *mine*." And with that, he left quickly.

Benjamin bowed to the young woman. "I'm sorry that scoundrel disturbed you," he told her, "but don't worry, you can enjoy your ice cream in peace. I'll watch from the doorway to make sure he doesn't come back."

"I'm afraid I've lost my appetite," she said. "Could you see me home? I'm afraid that man will follow me."

"It will be my honor, miss," Benjamin said. Once outside with the young woman, he looked around carefully to make sure that danger was nowhere to be seen, then offered his arm to her. She took his arm and smiled up at him. He said, "Thank you, miss."

"For what?" she asked. "It is I who should be thanking *you.* You saved me from great unpleasantness—possibly worse. As far as I'm concerned, you did a *great thing.*"

"If I've saved a damsel in distress, that certainly would be a great thing—and a wonder. I keep telling my mother that to do great things, one has to leave home. But just now, apparently, I've done a great thing, and I only had to travel seven miles to do it! It's for that—and for taking my arm—that I must thank *you.*"

She laughed, and asked, "Do mutual thanks cancel each other?"

"Oh no," he said, "they add to each other."

"In that case," she said, I'd like to tell you my name is Emily."

"But if our mutual thanks canceled each other," he asked, "what then?"

"I'd tell you my name anyway."

"And *his* name is Benjamin," Emily said excitedly later that evening, as Beatrice was brushing her hair while she sat before her bedroom vanity. "And he's a Lieutenant in the National Guard, and he said he wants to call on me!"

Beatrice continued brushing steadily, not missing a stroke. "If he's an officer in the National Guard," said Beatrice, "then he probably has money—more, at least, than the fireman. But I suppose you've noticed that."

"I couldn't have missed it. I didn't ask him where he comes from, but he volunteered that his family has a place in Bloomingdale."

"I see he wanted to impress you."

"I think so."

"Bloomingdale is a long way from Five Points."

"Of course it is," said Emily. "And Benjamin's family doubtless has thousands and thousands of times more money than Sean's."

"What does that mean to you?"

"I'll tell you what it does *not* mean, that Benjamin is thousands of times more the man that Sean is. It just means he's...*different*—that's all."

"Just different?"

"Look Beatrice, Benjamin is a charming and gallant officer who saved me from a nasty situation. At this stage, anything more is premature. Benjamin is just...*different.* He's not likely to humiliate me in public the way Sean did. He's better bred than that."

"Better bred—as if, somehow, more money means more manners?"

"Are you trying to pick a fight with me, Beatrice?"

"No indeed, child. I'm just trying to find out what's going on in that interesting mind of yours."

"I'm wondering myself. Let's just say that I want a change, and that's what Benjamin means to me—a change."

"Well, honey chile, if it's change you want, it's change you are certainly going to get."

"You disapprove of my feelings?"

Flames

"How could I approve or disapprove of anyone's feelings—least of all, yours? Better for me to step back and see what you'll do with them."

"Yes," said Emily, "what I will *do*—I'm eager to see that myself." She walked to the open window, and looked out at the city at night, where only a few dim lights could be seen. She lifted her eyes to the heavens, where, in contrast, a myriad of stars were brilliant in the night sky.

These stars seemed less important at the Livingston estate, whose great mansion seemed ablaze with lights of their own. Inside, in the gracious dining hall, Benjamin sat together with his mother Martha, her sister-on-law Abigail Livingston, and Abigail's ward, Katherine Greene. His mother chided her son: "We've been waiting supper for hours, Benjamin."

Benjamin frowned. "You shouldn't have waited, mother. I don't mind eating alone in the kitchen. You must have felt half starved; I'm sorry."

Abigail snorted. "Not sorry enough to keep you from doing it the next time, I'll wager."

"Probably not, Aunt Abigail. And there are likely to be many more next times. At least for a while—until I gain my object."

Katherine spoke up: "I gather you're busy falling in love again?"

Benjamin affectionately placed his hand on her arm. "As always, Katherine, you gather correctly," he said, smiling at her, "but this is not like the last time."

Abigail snorted again. "That's exactly what you *said* the last time."

"Ah, but this one is different."

"You said *that* the last time, too."

"What is she like?" asked Katherine. "She's pretty, I suppose?"

"Very pretty, but that's the least of it. She really transcends any words I could say about her."

"Now that *is* different" said Abigail. "You could hardly stop talking about the last one."

"You'll see for yourselves if I can gain her consent to come here."

"*Her* consent?" said his mother; "what about mine? Before the hussy sets one foot in this house, you're going to need *my* consent first."

"Whoa," said Benjamin, "we're getting ahead of ourselves, here. I have her permission only to come calling."

"And her father's permission, too, I suppose?" asked Martha.

"He could scarcely withhold it."

"Truly? And why is that?"

"I was of some service to her. They both have reason to be grateful to me—which, in a way, could be a problem. Gratitude is not what I want. And if gratitude is *all* there's likely to be, then everyone can stop worrying; I'll start appearing on time for supper."

"Until the next young lady comes along," said Abigail.

"If this doesn't work out, there may not *be* a next young lady. I may decide I've had my fill of love."

"That would be a pity," said Katherine.

For the first time, Abigail cracked a smile, with which she favored Katherine. "My sweet young ward," she said, "I wouldn't worry about it. He said *that* the last time, too."

Flames

Twenty-Two
I am *choosing well*

It was a morning in early December, and there was a nip in the air. Emily and Benjamin were walking, her arm in his, down one of the streets in the northern, more fashionable part of town. "Wasn't it fun," she said, "last night at Colonel Parker's?"

Benjamin beamed at her. "More than fun," he said. "For me it was gratifying to be the most envied man in the house, dancing with not only the most beautiful woman there, but also the loveliest dancer. Did Mrs. Okill teach you to dance the Lancers Quadrille that way?"

Emily laughed. "Who else? 'fiery thoughts, but fairy steps,' that was her teaching."

"Well, you put it to exquisite use last night."

"I tried—though sometimes it was hard to do and still keep up with you."

"Really?"

"Well, when you took my hand and strode forward to meet the opposite couple, you quite dragged me along with you!"

"Sorry. I've long since mastered the 'fiery thoughts' part, but I never quite got that 'fairy steps' thing."

"You're forgiven! You were very cute. And more than a few women told me how much they envied *me!*"

"Which means, I suppose, that, winsome as we seem to have been, we can expect many more such invitations—if we can stand it!"

"Perhaps it would do for us to be a tad less winsome," she said.

"Good idea. We could reverse the formula: we could have fairy thoughts but fiery steps. I could stomp around the room, while you'd stand in one place and glower."

"Glower?" she asked. "Is that a fairy thing?"

"Oh yes—if you're a wicked fairy."

"I see. One evening like that," she said, "and we'd be quite written out of the social season, which I wouldn't mind in the least if it meant I'd have more time to be alone with you. These past weeks have been wonderful. I can't tell you how grateful I am for the kindness you've shown me."

"Dear Emily, please don't speak of gratitude. If anyone should be grateful, it's I. Your taking my arm like this, and our walking with gentle steps together—*that* is the dance for me."

Emily thought: *that dance has certainly distracted me from thinking about a certain fireman.* But what she said was "you're very kind. And I wish there were more of a chance for our relationship to grow into…something meaningful."

"It's already meaningful to me."

"I think you know what I mean."

"Still thinking of Sean Dougherty?"

"I haven't seen him in eleven months," she said.

"Eleven whole months? It sounds like you've been counting them."

Is it so obvious? And am I merely playing with the affections of this kind man? It's not fair to him! "Benjamin, when I give my heart, I want to give it unreservedly, without qualification of any kind."

"There's no other gift I would accept."

Flames

"And you deserve no less. But right now, I'm not sure I *can* give it. And I don't want to lead you on." *Please God, give me the courage to send him away!*

"This sounds like my cue to take you home, and ask that you let me know—either way—when you are sure. Shall I take you home?"

I should say "yes." Just one word—why can't I say it?

Benjamin asked again: "Shall I take you home?"

"I wouldn't blame you for doing that."

"But would you like it if I stayed?"

Emily took a deep breath and thought, *here I go!* "Yes, I would like it," she sighed, "very much. But I'm not sure I'm entitled to ask it of you—to ask *anything* of you, for that matter."

"All you need do is ask. *That* entitles you, so far as I'm concerned. There's something troubling you..."

"Is it so obvious?"

"To me, it is. And what kind of a friend would I be to leave you alone with your trouble?"

"A good friend...a good friend..."

"But not so good a friend as I'd like to be. Emily, if you'd like to talk to me about...anything...then we don't have to go home. I'm here. You can talk to me now. Is it about Sean?"

"Not only about him. It's also about my father. When you met me, did you know my father's connection with slavery?"

"As soon as I knew who your father *was*. Your father's a very prominent financier."

"And weren't you disgusted?"

"Your father also uses a chamber pot. Should *that* disgust me? We all use one; it's a fact of life. But on the positive side, your father loves you more than life itself. Rather than remarry, he's dedicated everything he has, everything he *is,* to you. Yes, certainly he's involved himself in a sordid trade. He knows it. And to get through the day, he has to sell himself a bill of goods."

"How do you know?"

"Because the offer of actually becoming a slaver was more than he could stomach. And possibility of the neighbors knowing he was merely *visited* by a slaver embarrassed him so much that he put up with that rotter in his home for a quarter hour. Your father feels shame, Emily. That's a good sign that God's not finished with him yet."

"But in the meantime," said Emily, "there's all this money he's made off of slavery, all this tainted money. And I'm the beneficiary of it. Doesn't that taint *me*—all that poison money? What kind of dowry is *that?*"

Benjamin smiled down at her. "God kept King David from building the Temple, because his hands were covered with blood," he said. "But David's son Solomon built it handily. He inherited David's wealth, but not his blood guilt. Whatever your father's guilt may be, it need not pass to you."

"You're a very comfortable fellow to be around!" she said.

"'Comfortable' is a good start, but I want to be more to you than just a comforter."

"And I want more, as well."

"Emily, I must ask you: why don't you go back to him?"

"You seem to be pleading your rival's cause. Why?"

Flames

"I wish I knew. In the meantime, please answer me: why don't you go back to him?"

She drew herself up to her full five foot seven inches. "I'll never go back to him."

"Why not?

"I'm ashamed—and angry. He called me a spoiled hot-house flower—a Daddy's girl, no fit woman for a grown man."

"But these sound like words spoken in the heat of passion. Surely they can be forgiven?"

"I don't know if I *want* to forgive him."

"Indeed! Why not?"

"For one thing, he seems to be doing quite well without me."

"He doesn't know what he's throwing away."

"There's something else. I don't know if he wants me for myself, or for my father's money—tainted though it is. He *says* the money means nothing to him. But that's easy for him to say."

"You don't have the confidence to imagine that someone could love you for yourself alone, and not your money?"

"*Should* I have this confidence?"

"I know at least one person in the world who wouldn't care if you didn't have a penny—so long as you liked him."

"Have you stopped pleading your rival's cause, Benjamin Livingston?"

"Absolutely. Anyone who thinks you're no fit woman for a real man doesn't deserve to be taken seriously. I'm a real man I hope, and I *know* you're fit for me. My lovely Emily, I'm yours if you will have me."

She smiled at him. "I will," she said, "gladly." *And gratefully,* she added to herself. *Of course there should be more than gratitude;* I want *there to be more, and if I want it enough, there'll have to be more in time, no? I'll make* sure *there's more.* Then audibly, yet very quietly, she repeated, "gladly."

Seeing her apparently lost in thought, Benjamin said, "are you really sure, now? I want you to say yes because…because you *like* me, not because you're angry at someone else."

"Yes, I *am* sure, and I *do* like you, very much. If I'm angry at anyone, it's at myself for…wasting so much time."

"The time isn't wasted if you choose well."

"I *am* choosing well."

"Thank you."

"But my father will have to approve."

"I'd like to ask him, now!"

"Let's wait 'till he gets home from the office—it's only about six hours to go."

"That's a long time to wait!"

"Surely you don't want to interrupt him at his work? No one ever does *that.*"

Flames

Twenty-Three
Interruptions

Bender Finance: these words were on the second story of Thaddeus Bender's Nassau Street office building, and the office itself was on the second floor. It was staffed with half a dozen clerks, all working, standing up, at their respective ledgers. Thaddeus himself, however, was sitting behind his desk on a platform—10 feet square and 6 inches high. He was holding a quill pen and writing a letter, when the door suddenly opened and Jacques de La Tour strode in. "*Où est* Monsieur Bender?" he declaimed.

Thaddeus looked up. "In this country, Mister de La Tour," we are accustomed to people announcing their arrival by *knocking first.* It is considered polite."

"Ah, but in my line of work, *mon cher monsieur*," the last thing I think about is *la politesse*. It is not my style. You will forgive me, I'm sure."

"Don't count on it. But you have come to learn my answer to your proposal—yes?"

"*Bien sûr,* Monsieur!" What is your answer?"

"My answer is no—absolutely not."

"*Pourquoi pas?* You have turned down a fortune. I did not know bankers did that."

"Bankers do whatever the hell they feel like doing. Their reasons—*my* reasons—are none of your business. Let's just say that the farther I get from people like you—and from what you do—the better I like it."

Paul R. Cooper

De La Tour favored Thaddeus with a sour smile. "You have tried to humiliate Jacques de La Tour," he said; "that does take courage, Monsieur. I could choose to feel insulted, throw down my gage, and if you had the courage to pick it up, we could duel in New Jersey where the law isn't enforced so strictly as here. But that would give you the advantage of knowing when and where to expect me. That is not my style. Yes you have hurt me, deeply, and at our next meeting...on that day, monsieur, you will share my pain. When will it come, the day of pain? Who knows? Maybe in months. Maybe tomorrow. But I assure you: as it comes for everyone, *so it will come for you.* That is all you need to know for now," he said, as he walked to the door. Then he turned and said, *"n'est-ce pas?"* and left.

Immediately, a short, rotund clerk went quickly to Thaddeus and with a theatrically conspiratorial air, said: "Shall I follow him, boss—like I did with Sean Dougherty?"

"No, Egmont: this one you stay far away from," replied Thaddeus in an equally low voice. "But hush..." And he led Egmont into a back room.

Once there, Egmont continued, "But I found out lots about Sean—got a real line on his character. And he never knew I was spying for you."

"That's because Sean—as we found out—is completely without guile, and would suspect none from you or anyone else. But this de La Tour, on the other hand, is quite the opposite: he's dangerous—you'd be risking your life."

"So what? My life doesn't mean that much to me, nowadays."

"Really?" said Thaddeus. "Why would that be?"

164

Flames

"It's personal, boss."

"Well, I won't pry. Whatever your reasons, you're willing to give your all to help me, and that means a lot. Hm...I wonder...Egmont, I have an idea."

Almost in a whisper, Egmont said, "you're not saying you want me to *shoot* him, boss?! I fired a gun once when I was on the stage, but of course there were only blanks in it. Still, of a need, I suppose I could do target practice, and then we could see if—"

"You surprise me, Egmont," Thaddeus interrupted, "I'm beginning to think I don't really know you at all."

"Few people really know me, Boss. But don't worry. If you want me for dark purposes, I continue to be at your disposal."

"If I thought you could get away with it without implicating *me*, I'd consider it. But not this time. Still, there *is* something very helpful you can do."

"Anything, boss. You name it."

"I will. But first..." Thaddeus led Egmont into the main room, and raised his voice, loudly declaring to his office clerks, "We're closing early today, so you can all go home—I'll pay for the hours you miss. So everyone out—except Egmont, here. He and I have some private business."

When the office was cleared, Thaddeus said quietly, "All right, Egmont: I'll draft a letter, and you'll make a hundred or so copies of it—one to each of my business contacts. I'll give you the list—of all the bankers, all the substantial merchants, even the people in the slave trade—in short, a list of everyone who would like me in their debt. And the letter will

165

say that I would esteem it a great favor if they would refuse to have anything to do with Jacques de La Tour, if they would refuse to lend him money, refuse to hire him for any purpose, even refuse to rent him a room, or to be of the slightest assistance to him. For this great favor I would be exceedingly grateful, and deeply in their debt. When you have the copies ready, I'll sign them, and then you'll go out and deliver them. How does that sound?"

"Impressive!"

"Well, what do you expect—he threatened us!" A faint smile played on his lips. "No one should do that. Not to us. There are consequences."

"As you say, boss! Just give me the copy and the address list, and I'll start right away. Though I must say…"—and here Egmont affected a broad French accent—"Jacques de La Tour will be humiliated all ze more!"

Thaddeus smiled grimly. "I'm afraid so. I daresay we'll see him again."

At Megan Dougherty's house, Megan and Sean were at table, having tea. "What's your trouble, Sonny," she said, "you're seldom home at all, let alone so early."

"I wasn't feeling so well today, Ma, and I got Mr. Tappan to let me leave early."

"Not feeling so well? What's the matter?"

"Oh, I don't know. Maybe I'm getting sick or something. I've no strength. I just feel rotten."

"You're not takin' up with that young missy again, are you?"

Flames

"I haven't seen Emily in almost a year."

"That's a mercy. And a good riddance."

"I suppose so."

"You *suppose* so? I *know* so! She would have caused you nothing but grief."

"You would have made sure of that, wouldn't you, Ma?"

"If you're going to talk to me like that, why bother coming home for comfort?"

Sean looked at his mother a few moments. "That's a good question," he said.

"I met him at church, after services, in the old churchyard," Mrs. Gallagher said, in answer to no spoken question. She and her little family were sitting at table in Bender's first floor kitchen. Mrs. Simon and her family were there, too, but Mrs. Gallagher wasn't seeing them. She saw, rather, that old churchyard drenched in midday June sunshine, with Tiger Lilies and Forsythia exuberantly blooming. "My family had wanted me to notice someone else, a very tall, thin man," Mrs. Gallagher continued, "but I had my eye on a shorter fellow, a red head with broad shoulders and strong arms. He looked like someone who knew how to work, knew how to hold a woman—and liked doing both. There was never any question about us. We just knew. Right from the time we first met, Matthew and I just...we just *knew.* We took long walks together, and he never said much—I did most of the talking...but when his hands stirred, and his strong arms moved...they said everything I needed to know."

In the long moment that followed, knives and forks stopped moving, and their users held their breath. Finally a sigh from Mrs. Simon broke the silence. "I know what you mean," she said.

This was the first sentence that Mrs. Simon had spoken to Mrs. Gallagher since their tense initial meeting. Mrs. Gallagher woke from her day dream, and said, "May I ask how you met Mr. Simon?"

"We'd been singing in the choir for years," Mrs. Simon answered. "I'm a low alto, Joe is a tenor—Joe *was* a tenor...He was always singing, always whistling. My folks would invite him over, and right in the middle of dinner, sometimes without warning, he'd burst into a song. He'd do it no matter where he was...If Joe were here now, he'd be making music somehow or other...Anyway, my folks didn't know what to make of him, but I knew...Still, I told him, you shouldn't sing on the street, or even whistle in public—especially when whitey's around. You can get into trouble that way...And for God's sake, don't sing in the middle of the night. When everyone's in bed, it's too late to be singing. But he'd just smile and say, "lover, it's *never* too late to be singing"...Right.

"Someone said to me the other day, that I must miss Joe's music terribly. Well what I miss really, is *him.* Joe *was* the music."

Mrs. Gallagher reached across the table and covered Mrs. Simon's hand with her own. "I'm so sorry that this has happened to you...and in this way. It's unbearable."

With her other hand, Mrs. Simon covered Mrs. Gallagher's outstretched hand, and said "but you and I have to bear it all the same, don't we?"

Flames

"What choice do we have?" Mrs. Gallagher said.

The two women remained like that for a minute or so, while in the shadows, observing, Benjamin whispered to Emily, "Sean was right about you. You are an angel."

"Not true, not true," she whispered back. "But let's leave them."

And she led Benjamin into another room, where he said: "It *is* true, Emily, "you *are* an angel."

"No, no, please, Benjamin—I'm nothing like that."

"All my life I've been looking for glory for myself—and have never found it. But you have never looked for glory, and are radiant with it."

"You don't know, you don't know! I'm just an ordinary person, with too many fears, too many vanities to deserve much praise of any kind. I'm not glorious at all—and certainly no angel! You do me too much honor, Benjamin; your praise is lovely to hear; it helps me live with myself. But I fear you're sadly deluded."

"I was deluded when I sought military glory. But that sort of glory no longer means so much to me. What means a lot to me now is the heavenly act I've just witnessed, and the woman responsible—yourself. If this is delusion, permit me to continue in it."

"With or without my permission, you'll learn the truth all too soon, I'm afraid."

If the smiling Buddha at the back of the tavern was trying to tell Sean that the price of love is pain, he was wasting his time: Sean knew it already. He had a shot glass half full of

Paul R. Cooper

scotch, and more in a pint bottle to refill the glass when the need arose—which looked to be soon, judging by the whiskey's failure so far to numb him. He looked up and saw someone coming. *"Good God,"* he thought, *"it's Egmont—all I need!"*

Without asking permission, Egmont slumped onto the bench opposite Sean, who said: "Egmont, you look terrible!"

"Sean," Egmont croaked, "you might as well know that my real name is not Egmont, but *Yechezqel.*"

"What?"

"That's Ezekiel, in Hebrew. That's what my parents named me."

"In Hebrew?"

"I'm Jewish. Though I've tried to hide that fact ever since I came to this country."

There was a silence. Then Egmont continued, "I just got word from Germany that my father has committed suicide."

"Oh my God, I'm so sorry to hear it!"

"Thank you."

"What could have moved him to do such a thing?"

"Fifteen years ago, in Wurzburg, Germany, my mother was killed in the Hep Hep riots. He never got over it. I guess it finally became too much for him."

"Poor man! But somehow, you and he escaped the rioters?"

"We weren't there when it happened. My father had taken me to a carnival in another town—mother was a little under the weather, and said we should go by ourselves. While

Flames

we were away, the rioters—looking for any Jew they could lay their hands on—saw she was alone in the house, and...well..."

"Where were the police all this time?"

"They were actually trying to suppress the riot, and—to a large extent—they succeeded. But in my mother's case, they got there too late. There were about a half dozen men in the gang that raped her and strangled her to death. She had done nothing. Her only fault was that she was Jewish."

"Horrible."

"To destroy the evidence, they torched the house. Coming back, we saw the flames and wondered how close they were to our home. When we saw that it *was* our home, we whipped the horses into a gallop. But by the time we got there, the firemen had arrived ahead of us, and the police already had the gang members in custody. Very efficient, those Germans—even the gang members."

"I hear you."

"The firemen got my mother's body out of the house and had covered it with a sheet. I went to pull the sheet off her face, but the police went to stop me—it was no sight for a young person, they said. But I shouted, *I'm her only child!*

"They looked at my father for guidance, but he was frozen. So they drew down the sheet for me, and when I looked at her, I saw that the police were right—I shouldn't have looked. For now, when I think of her, I don't remember her the way she was in life. No. Instead, all I can bring to my mind is that...charred horror."

"Oh Lord," Sean said, "to have to go through that so young!

"My father and I were in shock. Some days later, when he could finally speak coherently, he said, "This is what happens when people know you're a Jew." And in the next few months he scraped together enough money to pay for one passage to America, and to send me over—alone. *Don't ever let anyone over there know you're Jewish*—those were the last words I ever heard him speak. Not that we didn't keep in touch. I'd hear from him occasionally; he would often move to a new city to see if he could make a new life for himself *there*, and he'd write me his new address, and always he'd say, *does anybody over there know you're Jewish? I myself can't hide my Jewishness over here, but there in America, you may have a chance. Don't disappoint me.*

"What a burden he placed on you," Sean said.

"Burden or not, I felt bound to follow my father's instruction. So I put on an act—I turned myself into a lapsed Lutheran, a jokester, longing for the stage. I became very good at it!"

"You *are* very good at it. But what a way to live—always in fear of being discovered."

"Fear is right. Ever since I got here, I've wanted to say Kaddish for my mother on each anniversary of her death. But I've been afraid to recite that prayer, because to say it, there have to be at least nine other men present, and those who saw me would know I'm Jewish. I couldn't take the chance. Now my father is gone, and I want to say Kaddish for him, too—whether or not it's proper to say it for a suicide. I want to recite Kaddish for them both!"

"Then recite it!" said Sean. "They deserve it, and you deserve it. Go do it! I would, if I were you."

Flames

"You would?"

"Sure—I'd follow my own religion, if I knew what the hell it was. But since you seem to know you're Jewish, go follow it. You'll be doing yourself a favor."

In Delmonico's Café Thaddeus and Mayor Lawrence were having their snack. "Have you noticed how cold it's been getting?" asked the Mayor. "Close to zero this morning, and it's only early December. At this rate, the winter is going to be a big challenge for us." The Mayor pulled out a gold pocket watch, and glanced at the time.

"Do you have another appointment?" Thaddeus asked.

"Not really. When I'm nervous, I keep checking the time for no good reason—which makes me more nervous. Right now, I'm wondering what problems there'll be from the big freeze coming on."

"Keeping everybody warm?" asked Thaddeus.

"There's that—though Pennsylvania coal is pretty cheap these days, thanks to the Canal. But a bigger challenge is to keep the city from burning down."

"Arsonists?"

"Unfortunately, there's always that, too. No—I mean the incompetents who don't know how to bank a stove fire, or patch an exhaust pipe, or detect leaking gas. They're the real danger."

"I know enough not to ask about building inspections—nobody wants 'em, and you can't afford 'em, anyway."

"Right. So as the temperature dips, more fires are going to go out of control. I keep thinking of the fire next time." The Mayor checked his watch again.

173

"Getting any sleep, nowadays, Cornelius?"

"Not really. And you, Thaddeus?"

"No. I'm worried about the fire *this* time."

The Mayor placed his hand on Thaddeus' arm. "My friend," he said, it's time for your guardian angels to rescue you."

"Oh really?" said Thaddeus. "And just how do I get them to do that?"

"You have to ask them, Thaddeus. That's always a good start."

"Easier said than done, Cornelius."

"Don't I know it, my friend."

Thaddeus and the Mayor left the restaurant together, shook hands genially, and went their separate ways, after which Thaddeus thought he saw, across the street, Jacques de La Tour seemingly absorbed in a newspaper. His first thought was to cross the street and challenge him: *Are you following me?* But then he thought it wiser to keep on walking and see whether he actually *was* being followed. After walking a block, he suddenly whirled around, but de La Tour was nowhere to be seen.

Flames

Twenty-Four

Someone far more attractive to kiss

At Thaddeus' house, a few hours later, the pocket doors were closed to partition the front parlor from the back. Benjamin was pacing back and forth in front parlor while in the back, Emily and her father were closeted in an intense discussion.

"Now that Benjamin has asked for my permission," he told Emily, "it's *you* I need to talk to. Compared to us, Benjamin's family is almost like royalty. To them we're nothing but contemptible shop keepers. Ben's marriage to you would be a real blot on their escutcheon."

"Thanks for the vote of confidence."

"I love you, Emily, and I wonder if you'll be happy under the uplifted noses of people only too eager to find fault with you, to prove that they were right about you and Benjamin wrong."

"So long as Benjamin loves me, I don't care—and neither should you."

Thaddeus gazed at her for what seemed to Emily to be a long time. "So," he said finally, "this is it, then? That man in the front parlor is the one who will take you away from me?"

Emily smiled. "Only so far as is seemly and appropriate, Daddy. I'll be his wife, but I'll always be your little girl."

For a few moments, Thaddeus was deep in thought. Then, having made his decision, he said to Emily: "Let me tell you this: long ago I put language in my will stating that upon my death, everything of which I stand possessed belongs to you, only to you, and *not* to any husband you might have. I

175

don't care what the lawyers may say—that money is for *your* control, and not for your husband's."

"Father, what are you talking about? What are you saying?"

"Emily my dear, this is my way of saying yes."

Emily and her father embraced, then she opened one of the pocket door partitions just wide enough for her to slip her slim body through and run to Benjamin, flinging herself into his arms as passionately, she hoped, as the heroines in her night table romances. "He says yes!" she cried, noticing that while she was happy, she wasn't feeling anything like the ecstasy that Sarah Cunningham said she'd experienced when she first learned of her father's approval. *Could Sarah have been exaggerating, or am I simply not happy <u>enough</u>?* She lifted her face to be kissed, and Benjamin gently supplied the kiss she seemed to be asking for. She looked searchingly into his eyes, and said, "kiss me again—*harder.*"

Again he complied, this time with more vigor, and she thought, *this is more like it—I think.*

Benjamin ended the kiss in order to gaze at her rapturously, and say, "my darling! Now I *know* you'll be all mine!" Then he hugged her fiercely, while she, aware that he could not see her face, allowed herself to think: *he loves me—that should be enough. Shouldn't it?*

Benjamin took a step back from her, his hands on her shoulders, his face so beaming with the pride of possession that Emily was relieved when the partition opening widened enough to accommodate the more substantial Thaddeus, who came through to be greeted by Benjamin's question: "We have your blessing, sir?"

"I just *told* you we did, silly!" said Emily to her fiancé.

Flames

"May God bless you both," said Thaddeus.

"How beautiful this is!" cried Benjamin. "As soon as I can tear myself away, I'll ride home and tell my mother the happy news."

"When you go, dear," said Emily, "please button up. It's getting awfully cold out there."

"I'll button, I'll button."

But when it came time for Benjamin to leave, Emily insisted on buttoning each of his coat buttons herself, "to make sure it's done right."

"When your mother hears the news," she said, "do you think she'll be pleased?"

"Of course she will," he replied, "she'd better be." Then he touched Emily on her shoulder. "Are *you* pleased, dear? Really pleased?"

"Of course I am," she said, making sure that her face reflected a happy serenity.

"How could you do this to me?" said Martha Livingston to her son, Benjamin. They were at her great mansion in Bloomingdale. With them were Abigail and Katherine. "I'll be the laughing stock of all New York," she said.

"Most New Yorkers will not even have heard of it, Mother."

"I'm talking about those who *matter*. Those with families, who wouldn't even consider allying themselves to a...a merchant, or whatever he is."

"The way you talk, I'm embarrassed to have asked Emily to become allied to *my* family. I'm embarrassed to have asked for a blessing from her father."

Paul R. Cooper

"That wretched fellow. As we speak, he's probably gloating over his step upward in life, being linked to the Livingstons."

"Quite the opposite. I overheard him urging Emily to reconsider the match, lest she be made miserable by her in-laws' attitude. "Uplifted noses" was the expression he used, I believe. Sometimes I think it epitomizes you, mother."

"Ungrateful child. I have given you everything"—

"I hope *not!*"—

"*You* hope...**you** hope?!" cried Martha. "*I* had hoped for a far better match for you. Katherine would have proved far more suitable—in education, in culture, and in *breeding*" not to mention...

But Benjamin had turned to Katherine, and it was at her he gazed while he said: "Katherine Greene is a lovely woman, mother; she is better than you can even imagine, better than any of us deserves, and I hope our friendship will last our whole lives—I'm quite fond of her." Katherine lowered her eyes. "But I'm in love with someone else, that's all."

Martha replied, "You talk of making Emily miserable. You are making all of *us* miserable, Benjamin—*me* especially!"

"Mother, I was bound to make you miserable, some day, by marrying *anybody*. The truth is that in your eyes *nobody* could be good enough for me—good enough, that is, for *you*. If I married Katherine here, you would find even in *her* some fault or other to harp on. As for the misery you say I've inflicted on Katherine and Abigail, all I can say is...I'm sorry."

"Then you've finished?"

"No. Here it is: Emily Bender and I are engaged to be married. To celebrate our engagement, I'm bringing her here to meet you. If you cause her even the slightest pain or discomfort, you may never see me again. Is that perfectly clear? Do you have any questions?"

There was a silence, which Katherine broke by speaking very softly: "May I ask a question?"

"Of course, Katherine."

"When are you bringing her?"

"Why, as soon as Mother can have a decent supper prepared; let's say in two days—this coming Wednesday."

"Out of the question," Martha snapped. "A feast to welcome your betrothed is worth more than two days preparation time! The earliest I'll agree to is a *week* from this coming Wednesday."

"All right—we'll have it *then:* Wednesday, December 16th. That should satisfy all objections."

"All except one: this December weather," Katherine said quietly. "It's getting very cold. Might it not be *too* cold for Emily? Might it not be better for her to wait until it warms up a little?"

Benjamin said, "You know, you're right. That's very thoughtful of you, Katherine, and typical—you're a good friend. I'll ask Emily. If she wants to wait, then we'll wait." He turned to Martha. "Otherwise, Mother, let it be a week from this coming Wednesday—the 16th. I'll let you know."

And with that, he strode out of the room and out of the house, closing the door behind him—very firmly.

At long last, Abigail found her voice: "He didn't even kiss you goodbye, Martha."

Of course not," replied her sister-in-law, "his mind is fixed on someone far more attractive to kiss."

"Very much more attractive, I'm afraid," Katherine murmured.

Martha rose, went to Katherine, put her hand on her shoulder, and said, "are you all right, my dear?"

"I'll be all right. Benjamin is happy; that's the main thing. Emily sounds like a lovely person."

"Sounds is right," muttered Abigail. "We haven't even *met* her yet."

"Oh, I don't doubt that she is everything Benjy says. She'll bring him joy; I don't doubt it for a second." For a moment Katherine was lost in her thoughts, then she added, "Of course, if joy could have come *to both of us together*—Benjy and me—it would have been a dream...but I guess that was too much to hope for. It's time to wake up."

Flames

Twenty-Five
They're only animals

When Sean stepped out of the rain to enter the tavern, he thought he could make out what seemed like a shadowy apparition sitting where he liked to sit—at the table in the dark corner presided over by the helplessly smiling Buddha. A few steps confirmed the presence of a man dressed in black. Sean cursed under his breath. A quick glance told him that the tavern was unusually full that rainy evening, that he would not have the luxury of drinking alone, and that he might as well see if the man in black would mind company. He approached him.

"Is this your seat, *monsieur?*" said the man. "*Pardonnez-moi!*"

"It's true I'm used to sitting here," Sean said, "but I don't own the table, and I'd be grateful if you wouldn't mind company."

"*Bien sûr,*" please join me."

As he heard those words, Sean thought he detected an unsavory odor emanating from the man, but he didn't know how he could suddenly change his mind without appearing rude. "Perhaps for a short while," he said, sitting down.

"Aha!" said the man, "*vous sentez une odeur désagréable.*"

"Huh?"

"I smell bad. Haven't bathed in weeks. That's not my style, but...*Je suis sans-abri.*

"You're *what?*"

181

"Homeless. I sleep in the street. Can't find work."

"What kind of work do you do?"

"I'm a...a ship captain."

"And you can't find work? Nowadays there's a big demand for ship captains. They're advertising for them everywhere—business must be booming."

"But not for me. It's claimed that on my last voyage, I lost too much cargo. It spoiled."

"Spoiled?"

"Died. They claim 20 percent died, but they lie. It was no more than 15 percent."

"What sort of cargo do you ship?"

"Animals. Hundreds of them in each voyage. On my last voyage there was much sickness—like a plague. 15 percent died. It's a pity, but after all, they're only animals."

"What sort of animals?"

"Wild animals. From the jungle."

"Like lions and tigers?"

"Something like that. And for the loss of a few wild animals, no one will hire me! There is a cabal against me, and when I find out who's behind it, then I—"

"Take it easy, Mister—no need to run off half-cocked! I know what you need—something to eat. Let's get the waitress over here and order something good for your—"

"Attendez Monsieur!" The man in black looked like he was about to explode. "You walk on dangerous ground! You come very close to insult!"

"I meant no insult. All I meant was to offer some—"

Flames

"Be careful! *WHY* have you offered this food?"

"You want the simple truth?"

"Your life depends on it, Monsieur."

"The truth is that I was inspired by my girl friend's example. My *ex*-girl friend. If she were here, she'd be quick to offer you a meal. Her idea is to help those who need help. She is an angel, and I'm still trying to learn from her."

"This angel, as you call her, has just saved your life. *Écoutez-moi!* monsieur: My name is Jacques de La Tour. I accept charity from no one. What I need, I take. It is raining out, so I took shelter. When I need food, I take that, as well. If you want to live, offer me nothing."

"Mister de La Tour, you're a very proud man."

De La Tour favored Sean with a wan smile. "You've noticed this?"

Flames

Twenty-Six
December 16, 1835

In the front parlor of Thaddeus' house, Benjamin bestowed on Emily's lips a very light and chaste kiss. "My angel," he said.

"Dear Benjamin."

"Tonight we're to go to my mother's house," he told her. "But it's so frigid out, I wouldn't blame you for postponing it. If we do postpone, I'll spend a few hours with you here before I return."

"But haven't they gone to great effort to prepare the supper?"

"The *servants* have made that effort, true enough. But as for Mother, Abigail and Katherine, they know that because of the weather we might have to cancel at the last moment. So if we don't show up, they are to go on with the supper without us."

"I don't like that idea," Emily said. "A week ago we promised them, and I like to keep my word."

"Even if it's colder than the bottom ring of Hell? Do you have enough winter wear to keep you warm?"

The pocket partition doors opened behind them, and Thaddeus entered, burdened with a great pile of fur-lined wraps, coats and boots. "Of course she does," said he, "do you think I'm the kind of father who would let his daughter get cold?" Thaddeus dumped the wraps on one of the front parlor sofas. "Of course, I'd prefer to keep her warm and snug at home, but if she's determined to make the trip, then far be it from me to stand in her way—we'll go."

Paul R. Cooper

In Benjamin's closed carriage were Benjamin, Thaddeus, and Emily, all riding to the Livingston Estate. Thaddeus looked out the window at the passing scenery; Benjamin closely regarded Emily, while she, eyes downcast, was seeing only images from the past—the fire company race, the visit to the burnt out houses, to Sean's mother, and to the widow Gallagher—but always returning to the passionate kiss she shared with Sean. Seeing her so abstracted, Benjamin asked if she was all right, was she warm enough; she replied that she was fine, thank you, and returned to her musing, which was terminated, abruptly, when Benjamin's voice announced, "We're here!"

Though liveried servants were rushing to assist the passengers, Benjamin leaped down to help Emily alight from the cab. When she stood on the metal step, he reached up and was about to lift her bodily from the cab, when she said, "that's all right, Benjamin, I can manage. All I need is your hand." He gave it; she alighted deftly, and then, with his arm around her, he led her to the front door, allowing the servants to try to assist with Thaddeus' getting out, a service which he politely declined.

In the foyer of the great house, Martha, Abigail and Katherine greeted their guests with expressions of welcome intermixed with exclamations of how cold they must have been on the trip: their coats were freezing! In this rush of activity, Katherine found time to whisper in Abigail's ear, "she's so beautiful!" Servants helped them off with these wraps, and they were led to the great Dining Hall.

Martha sat at the head of the table, Thaddeus opposite her at the foot, on the third side of the table sat Benjamin next

186

Flames

to Emily, while opposite them sat Abigail next to Katherine. Liveried servants—all blacks—arrived with various courses and took them away, while the Livingstons and their guests attempted conversation. Abigail began: "We hear that you're a banker, Mr. Bender. What sort of banking do you do?"

"All kinds," he replied vaguely. "Whatever is needed, I do it."

"But that Southern connection," Abigail pursued. "Isn't it...worrisome?"

"No more than for most bankers," he said. "To make a living, I must do what I know. Certainly it would be more pleasant to spend all my time listening to music or reading poetry, but financial pressures won't let me."

"Oh yes of course," said Abigail, "financial pressures."

"Exactly. So I'm forced to sell my time as dearly as I can. That doesn't leave me much time for music or poetry, but I work hard so that Emily can have plenty of time for both, if she chooses."

"Oh, Miss Bender," said Katherine, do you know Wordsworth? He's one of my favorites."

"Mine too, and—if you don't mind—I'd like it if you called me Emily."

"With pleasure. Do you know much of Wordsworth, Emily?"

"I know some. And at Mrs. Okill's school, we had to choose one of his poems to recite from memory."

"Which did you choose?"

"*I wandered lonely as a cloud.*"

"Oh, please do recite it for us, Emily."

And Emily recited it—beautifully.

"That was probably the finest account of that poem I have ever heard," Katherine breathed. "I do hope we shall be friends, Emily."

"That would give me great pleasure," Emily replied.

"You do seem to have learned it well, Miss Bender," said Martha. "Which is all the more remarkable, considering you learned it at one of those finishing schools whose main aim is to make young women more attractive to prospective husbands, an aim which in this case appears to have succeeded."

"My mother," said Benjamin, "has a unique sense of humor, but it's an acquired taste. She means well, but sometimes it's best to ignore her completely."

"Why not change the subject?" said Thaddeus. "The Erie Canal has been running for ten years, and has made New York City the capital of finance and business. We can connect easily, cheaply, to the American interior. That gives us an enormous advantage. No other American city comes close."

"Yes," said Benjamin, "the Canal has been very important in this. But you mustn't forget our natural harbor—deeper and more protected than any other harbor I've heard of. Ship captains naturally want to come here."

"Also because there are lots of business innovators here," said Thaddeus.

"And lots of cheap labor—you mustn't forget that," said Katherine. "I can't think of a place with a greater disparity between the very rich and the very poor."

"Scripture says that the poor we always have with us," Abigail offered.

Flames

"But ours are *so* poor," said Katherine. "I've *seen* how they live. No wonder there are so many riots. The wonder is that there are not more of them."

"What makes it worse are the continual fires," said Emily. "Building codes are poor and what codes exist are un-enforced. And the water system is terrible—not enough hy-drants and not enough water to supply them. We had two big fires last night. If, God forbid, we have another tonight, we might run out of water."

"Where did you learn all that?" asked Martha. "Surely not at Miss Okill's?"

"No," Emily said, "not at Miss Okill's."

"Where then?"

"From a fireman."

"A fireman!" chorused Abigail and Martha.

"A fireman—truly, Emily?" said Thaddeus.

"Yes, Father. From a fireman."

Martha turned to Thaddeus. "Do you know about this, Mr. Bender?"

"Mrs. Livingston," said Thaddeus, "If I said I had no idea, what would you think of me?"

"I'd say you were sadly deficient in your duty as a par-ent."

"And you'd be right."

"Well *I* know about it," said Benjamin, "and I can tell you it's perfectly innocent."

But Martha wouldn't let go. "All the same," she said, "I'd like to inquire: just what were you doing talking to a fireman, young lady?"

"Learning things. He was a friend of mine—for a while. He taught me a lot."

"What did you learn from him?" asked Katherine.

"That I needed to grow up."

Katherine said, "That must have been some fireman."

"He was. He is."

"I envy you," Katherine murmured, "it must have been very exciting. Did you go to a fire?"

"No, thank heavens. Since our house burned down two years ago, I've had an aversion to fires—more than that, really. To tell the truth I've been terrified of them. I had hoped that my fireman would help me get over this, but we weren't friends long enough." Emily laughed a little, then said, "when I hear there's a fire, I'd just as soon be anywhere else."

"I don't blame you," Katherine said.

"There'll be a chance to go to one tonight," said Thaddeus, pointing to the window.

They looked where he was pointing, and then ran to the window.

"Oh my God," cried Benjamin, "it looks like the whole city is afire!"

"I have to get down there," said Thaddeus, "I have a business there."

"Oh yes, of course," said Abigail, "a business."

"Oh Lord!" cried Emily, "I have to go with you, Father: I too have...business down there—unfinished business."

"We three will go together," said Benjamin. "I'm not letting you out of my sight, Emily."

"Good!" she said. "Make sure you don't; That looks like a huge fire—I'm not sure I'm brave enough to face it by myself."

"But what about supper," Martha complained, "it's taken days to prepare it!"

Flames

"I beg your pardon, Mrs. Livingston," said Thaddeus, "but we must postpone the pleasure. New York is burning."

Emily, Benjamin, and Thaddeus were back in Benjamin's carriage, whose two horses were racing to the city. Emily said to her father, "I suppose you'll want to know why I never told you about the fireman."

"Well you did, you know—at the very beginning. You said you had fallen in love with one, and I tried to dissuade you from pursuing it. My dear, I saw that I hadn't convinced you, but the only way I could prevent you from seeing him would be to lock you up, and I had no taste for it. Had your mother's family done that to *me*, you wouldn't be here, so I refused to do it to you. Still, I kept an eye on you."

"How did you do that?"

"A father has his resources," said Thaddeus, summoning to his mind an image of Egmont in manic mode, eager as a bloodhound to track the quarry. "Must I tell you *everything?*"

"I wish you'd had the courage to tell me about the slave trade."

A shocked Thaddeus, looking as if she had just slapped him in the face, managed to say, evenly, "The *cotton* trade, Emily. There's a difference."

"Not much of one, in my view."

"I knew that would be your view—an idealistic young woman like yourself. So I postponed telling you. But I knew I would have to tell you *sometime*, before you heard it from others."

"That's exactly how I *did* hear it."

"From your fireman, no doubt?"

"No doubt."

"And likely, that fireman is your unfinished business?"

"More than likely."

The pitch of Thaddeus' voice rose slightly: "May I ask, Emily, what unfinished business with him is proper for a young woman who's engaged to be married?"

"I'd like to know that, too," said Benjamin quietly, "if you don't mind my asking."

"I think you may *already* know part of it, Benjamin. Didn't I tell you that Sean and I parted on bad terms?"

"Yes you did. I'll never forget the day you told me about it."

"Well, I regret my parting words to him—especially now that he's in danger."

"Are you sure he's fighting this fire?" Thaddeus asked.

"A brave man like that, and a fire like this," Emily said, "he can be nowhere else!"

Grasping the nozzle end of a hose—that's indeed where Sean was, directing its stream against a wall of flame. But the air was so cold and the wind so fierce that most of the water was blowing back at him in the form of sleet, and Sean was covered with so much ice that he looked like a stalagmite with legs.

"Had enough, Chief?" said Timothy, who, with Patrick, was helping Sean manipulate the hose. "Let me spell you."

"Are you sure you're ready? You have about as much ice on you as I do."

"Not quite," said Timothy, "and I'm fine. But you may *not* be unless you let us rotate."

"You sold me," Sean said, handing the nozzle to Timothy, and taking his place behind Patrick, who had moved forward to be the next to hold the nozzle when it should become necessary to spell Timothy.

"Only one blessed hose to fight this blaze?" cried Patrick, "it's pitiful!"

"I know it," said Sean. "But with almost everything frozen—hydrants, hoses, and engines—what do you expect?"

"Do you think we could have a bit of that brandy, Chief?" asked Patrick.

"We're supposed to save it for the engine, lest it freeze up," said Sean.

"Yeah, but if *I* don't have a bit of it right now, I might freeze up, too!"

"I know what you mean, Pat. But stay tough for as long as you can."

"We're *all of us* staying tough, Chief," shouted Timothy, "but we can't do a thing against this monster! At the rate it's going, it's going to level the city! I hope somebody has a fall-back plan in mind."

"Don't worry!" cried Sean. When they figure out a fall-back plan, they'll tell us."

Meanwhile Mayor Lawrence, Charles King (the editor of the New York American), and James Hamilton (Alexander's third son), were among those trying to figure out a fall-back plan. They were standing on the shore of the East River, which was frozen solid. Several hoses were placed through holes cut in the ice, but firemen could be seen pumping only one engine. The other engines had been abandoned.

A half dozen firemen were attempting to cut more holes in the ice. "What good will this do?" said Hamilton. As soon as the water gets in the hoses, it will freeze as it has almost everywhere else, and seize up the engines."

"It would have been bad enough had the hoses been dry," said King, "but because of the two fires last night, what water remained in the hoses froze there, even before this latest fire. Our usual methods won't work here—we're going to have to try something else."

"What do you suggest?" Lawrence asked.

King was quick with his response: "Mr. Mayor, you should blow up some buildings and create firebreaks. If you don't, this monster will move North and West and devour everything on Manhattan Island."

"If I blew up buildings I'd be destroying private property," said the Mayor.

"A very small amount," said King, "compared to the property you'd be saving. You'd be saving the city."

"But this has never been done in New York State," the Mayor said.

"Still, there are state laws that provide for it," said Hamilton. "They were passed in 1806 and 1813, and not only do they authorize the destruction of buildings, but they provide compensation to the buildings' owners."

"Just what I need at a moment like this," the Mayor growled, "a lawyer!"

"With all due respect, Mr. Mayor," said Hamilton, "at this moment a lawyer may be precisely what you do need."

"Gentlemen," said Cornelius Van Wyck Lawrence, "If there are law suits, I and I alone will be the target. I'm not saying yes, yet. I have to think about it."

"Well, Mr. Mayor, don't take too long," said Charles King. "There are firemen out there risking their lives."

Flames

Sean, Timothy, and Patrick found themselves on the roof of a four-story building, having been ordered up there by Chief Engineer Gulick, in the desperate hope that with their single hose they might be able to wet down the roof of that building enough to keep it from catching fire from neighboring buildings already ablaze. "How long do we stay up here?" asked Timothy.

"Until Gulick tells us to come down," said Sean. "If we can keep this building from catching fire, that will be a big thing."

"Well, *I* don't see any flames up here—do you?" said Patrick. "If we really do stop the fire up here—we'll make the papers, don't you think?"

"It would be wonderful—that it would," said Sean, "but don't get your hopes up too high. This building might still catch fire—even if we didn't see it up here on the roof."

"Well I sure hope they're paying attention down there," said Patrick. I'm not eager to be roasted for dinner."

At that moment, they heard someone using a speaking trumpet to call to them.

"What did he say?" asked Patrick.

Sean moved to the edge of the roof. ***"WHAT DID YOU SAY?"*** he bellowed.

This time the voice came more clearly: **"The building's afire! Get the hell off that roof—now!"**

"Now he tells us!" Sean cried. "Go ahead, guys—down the stairs with you—*fast!* I'll bring up the rear." And the three men raced down the narrow, wooden stairwell only to find the third floor staircase blazing.

"Mother of God!" shouted Timothy, "what are we supposed to do now—jump from the third floor?"

At that moment a large tongue of flame leaped up as if to lick Timothy, who jumped back, shouting, "Jesus!"

"Out of the way—let me get there," said Sean, who moved to the window and then looked down. Then he raised his booted foot and with three kicks demolished the window.

"We're going to jump, are we?" said Timothy, crossing himself.

"No, no, Timmy, they've put a ladder there—right below the window—you didn't notice it. You guys go first—quick!"

So first Timothy, then Patrick sprang down the ladder, followed by Sean—just in the nick of time—for as he placed one foot on the ladder, an enormous tongue of flame roared out of the window, as if hungry for him.

When the three of them were on the ground, Timothy said, "Mother Mary, that was close!"

"Look on the bright side," said Sean. "The ice is fairly melted off us—and that without the fiery beast having us for supper. Not yet, anyway."

In the carriage, Emily was shaking her head. "When I think that something might happen to Sean," she said, "oh God! If something should happen to him without his having heard how sorry I am to have said what I did—I can't stand it!" For a moment she covered her face with her hands. Then she uncovered it, and looked out the window. "Oh Lord—look at the sky! It's getting redder and redder—like we're driving down into...into Hell! So be it. I have to find him—even if...it's in...the pit of the flames."

Flames

"Are you going to be all right?" Benjamin asked.

"I'm a little...short of air. But don't worry. Just...stay by me, Benjamin. I can do this if I...have you to hang on to. Stay close—and don't worry—I keep my promises."

Benjamin took her hand. "You are a principled woman, and I love you. We'll find him together."

As the carriage approached downtown, it seemed to slow down. "Why are we slowing?" asked Emily.

Thaddeus replied, "apparently, the horses don't like approaching this hell any more than we do."

"Let me see what I can do," said Benjamin, "but you'd better hold your coats tight around you—I'm going to open the top portal." He slid the portal hatch back into its well; a frigid blast roared in as he stuck his head through the opening. "Marcus," he called, can you get more speed out of these horses? Whip 'em if you have to."

"Very good, Master Livingston," came the driver's voice through the opening.

After Benjamin closed the portal, the passengers heard the sound of Marcus's vocal urging, and a few whip snaps, then felt the pace of the journey pick up.

"It's amazing what those horses will do with a little persuasion," said Benjamin.

"We three have...our persuasions, too," said Emily, gasping a bit. "More than a little."

The carriage stopped at Thaddeus' office, on Nassau Street where one could see, a few blocks down the road at Wall Street, a wall of flame towering skyward. Tearing his eyes away from the awful sight, Benjamin noticed that Thaddeus' office was right next to the offices of the American Anti-Slavery Society. "Look who's next door," he said. "Ironic."

"Yes," said Emily, "very." She directed a look at her father. "I wonder...how you could...stand it, Father," she said, struggling for breath.

"They do their business, and I do mine," replied Thaddeus, not very amused. "Look children: there's a nice warm stable next door. We'll tell the driver to put the horses in there. Then I'll see to some of the records in my safe, and put them in the carriage. It won't take but a minute or two."

"We understand, Father. Benjamin and I...will be going ahead. Will you wait for us...until we return?"

"Of course. But I'm amazed that you want to get closer. Even at this distance, that fire is....I wonder you're not terrified."

"I am...awfully. But Benjamin...will protect me." Breathing heavily, she closed her eyes, and Benjamin put a protective arm around her.

"And who will protect *him?*"

"May the Lord protect us all," said Benjamin.

As they alighted from the carriage, they saw emerging from the Anti-Slavery Society offices a couple of men who told them that the frigid weather had rendered most of the fire engines useless, and that the only thing most of the firemen could do was help remove merchandise from the warehouses.

Emily pounced greedily on this news. "This means Sean...may be at Tappan's right now!"

"Yes," said Benjamin, "it's a good place to start. Lead the way."

"You've been there before, Emily?" asked her father.

"Yes. I'll explain later...we'll *all* have...some explaining to do. Meanwhile, you carry on...leave us...and take care of business." By this time, Emily was panting.

Flames

"It'll take only a couple of minutes," Thaddeus said. "Then we can go together."

"No, no, Father...we'll go ahead...you can meet us at Tappan's."

"I know where it is," said Thaddeus. "As soon as I'm done, I'll run to it."

"Be careful, Father. If we don't meet up...we'll all meet back here." With both hands she grabbed Benjamin's right arm. He placed his left hand over one of hers, and gripped it hard. "Hold on tight, Benjamin," she gasped, "here we go..."

Benjamin and Emily, their eyes widened and their hairs bristling, headed southwest down Nassau Street, the fierce Northeast wind behind them.

When they got to the corner of Wall and Broad Streets, they saw some dozen men and women running in and out of stores, stealing whatever they could carry away. Some tried to conceal the items by stuffing them under their wraps, and some didn't even bother with concealment, either because the items were too large to conceal, or they figured the emergency was so extreme that nobody would care. One of them—a middle aged man—confronted the pair and shouted, "What are you staring at? You've never seen stealing before? Of course you have—but you swells do it with pen and ink and call it business. Now it's our turn. And it's about time!" And he ran off.

Meanwhile, some falling sparks had managed to ignite a few flames on the shoulder of Emily's coat. "Oh my God, Emily," cried Benjamin, "your coat's afire!"

"*Oh no!* Can you put it out? Help me!"

199

But Benjamin was already swatting the flames with his hat, and in short order had extinguished them. "The fire's out," he said, "but your coat is ruined."

"Do you think I care?" she said. "I can always...replace a coat. But that was a scare."

"Do you want to turn back?" Benjamin said.

"NO!" she cried. "I can still move...let's press on!"

And press on they did. Somehow, Benjamin and Emily made it to the corner of Wall Street and Pearl: Tappan's warehouse was now in sight. It was further down on Pearl Street, diagonally across the street from where the blaze had started. It had not yet reached Tappan's warehouse, though a warehouse next to it was already in flames. Tappan and some helpers—including a number of black men—were removing goods from his warehouse and flinging them into the center of Pearl Street where it widened to form Hanover Square.

Jacques de La Tour appeared, a black hole in the midst of Hell. He called out, "you niggers, why bother slaving for the Tappan brothers? After tonight, they and their warehouse will be ashes. Why should you join them in the ash heap?"

The blacks paused in their efforts, intimidated. But Sean stepped up and confronted de La Tour: "Who the hell are you to tell these men to stop working?"

"*Et qui Diable êtes*-vous, *mon cher ami*, to risk their lives in the first place?"

At this point the wind picked up and a large ball of flaming material blew off a roof and into Hanover Square, setting all the goods there on fire. Arthur Tappan rushed out to call to his workers, "It's not safe here anymore, men—let's get the rest of the stuff out the back onto Water Street—I know a safe place there." And all the workers went into the warehouse; Sean started to follow them, but stopped when he heard, then *saw* an overjoyed Emily, running to him with Benjamin close behind.

"Sean," she cried, "Sean! thank God you're all right!"

"Emily! I'm so glad!" he cried, embracing her. "But what are you doing here? And who is this man?" he said, indicating Benjamin.

"Her fiancé," said Benjamin. "We are to be married."

"You...he...?"

"Aha!" cried de La Tour, *"merveilleux! La femme, le fiancé, et le petit ami rejeté!"* He laughed sardonically.

At this point, Thaddeus, running full tilt, rounded the corner, and ran towards them. "Emily!" he cried.

"Daddy!"

"Parfait!" crowed de La Tour, *"Enfin—toute la famille des hypocrites!"* He whipped out his pistol. *"Now, in my vengeance, NOW* you shall see the style of Jacques de La Tour: there are four of you, but only two bullets in this, Messieurs. How shall I aim them? Well of course: at the treasure *Daddy* loves the most!" He leveled the pistol at Emily.

Quickly, Thaddeus put his daughter behind him, stepping in front of her, and both Sean and Benjamin rushed de La Tour. Sean was first; the shot that felled him and Emily's scream seemed to come almost at the same instant; meanwhile Benjamin flung himself at de La Tour, going for the gun which the Frenchman was trying to aim at Thaddeus. Benjamin was in good shape, but to deflect de La Tour's aim was all he could do: *how strong this Frenchman was!* Meanwhile, de

La Tour, with his other hand, was reaching for a switchblade knife whose cutting edge had just flashed open when the gun went off, harmlessly, in the air, freeing Thaddeus to race forward and seize de La Tour's stabbing arm before he had a chance to hurt Benjamin. With the convulsive strength of a tiger, de La Tour tore himself away from the two men, and, knife in hand, glared at them like a cornered beast. He lunged at Thaddeus, who, with surprising nimbleness, ducked out of his way. Meanwhile, Benjamin had wrapped his heavy wool scarf around his left arm. "Leave him to me, Mr. Bender," he said, "he's mine!" Benjamin advanced to close with de La Tour, who, having decided that discretion was the better part of valor, turned and ran into the street towards Hanover Square, when another giant fireball blew off the roof, landed on the Frenchman, and set him on fire. For the first time in his life, de La Tour, now ablaze, was a source of light.

Meanwhile Emily had run to the prostrate Sean. "He's alive! He's alive! Get help!" she cried.

At this point the Mayor appeared. "What are you mad people doing here?! Get out while you can; this place is dangerous!"

"More than you know, Cornelius," said Thaddeus. "But this fireman is hurt. Can you spare a couple of others to help us get him to my house?"

And the Mayor gestured to some firemen to come assist. As the firemen were running towards them, the Mayor said, "To make a firebreak, I've decided we're going to have to blow up some buildings, and you folks really don't want to be here anymore." By this time, the firemen were kneeling with Benjamin to raise up Sean.

Flames

Right about then, James Hamilton was racing up the stairs toward the entrance of the Merchants' Exchange building, while structures all around it were in flames. As he took the stairs two at a time, he encountered a man who recognized him. "James!" cried the man, "what are you doing here?"

"I've come to save the statue of my father, if I can."

"We've tried that, James, but it's too late; this building's finished."

"It can't be!" shouted James, "it's built like an armory! Let me by—I've got to see what I can do."

"You fool! Do what you have to, but I'm getting out of here."

And so James rushed in, only to see, as he approached, the dome start to collapse on the celebrated statue, the head of which, hit by falling lumber, was struck off its body to be smashed to bits on the pedestal. At this point, the few people left in the building now rushed out of it, and James Hamilton joined them. Once in the street, someone shouted to him, "if this fire can take down the Merchants' Exchange, what hope has the rest of the city?"

"Our only hope is to create a firebreak by blowing up some buildings," Hamilton shouted back. Intrigued, the man came closer to Hamilton, who continued, "I've persuaded the Mayor to collect all the gunpowder there is in Manhattan, and bring it to 48 Exchange Place. We'll see what we can do there."

Somewhere near 48 Exchange Place, the fire had become so intense that sparks were now coming down like rain, and copper was melting on the roofs and dripping off them in large, molten globules. Through this hell three men—James Cox, Uzziah Wenman, and a Watchman—were carrying a barrel of gunpowder which was leaking the explosive onto the ground. They saw someone rushing by with a blanket, and Wenman called for him to stop. "But this blanket is mine," said the passerby, I didn't steal it."

"I don't care whose it is," said Wenman, "but if I can't have it to wrap this barrel of gunpowder, we may all be blown to pieces!" The passerby gave up the blanket, and helped the soldier wrap the barrel. "Now, if we can just get this powder to 48 Exchange," said Wenman, "we may yet put a stop to this beast."

A few minutes later, at 48 Exchange Place, the men carrying the barrel were met by the Mayor, by Chief Engineer James Gulick, and by James Hamilton. The Mayor said to Gulick, "As Chief Engineer, Mr. Gulick, it is your duty to fire this powder and blow up this building."

"My business is with water," said Gulick, "not with gunpowder."

"There *is* no water," cried the Mayor; "if there were we could douse the building and hope to stop the fire that way. But since we can't, we must resort to gunpowder, and hope to create a fire block—otherwise the whole city may be lost!"

"I must warn you, Mr. Mayor, that if you blow up people's property, you risk a lawsuit."

"And if I default on my duty as Mayor, I risk far worse!" He looked at Uzziah Wenman. "Wenman, do you know how to bring down a building?"

"I've never done it, Mr. Mayor, but I think I know how."

"Go ahead, then—you and the other two."

"I might as well join 'em, since I arranged for the powder," said Hamilton.

Flames

"Go ahead, Hamilton," said the Mayor. And while the three men headed for the building, Hamilton stayed on the street to gather materials for a fuse: a bolt of fabric, some camphene, and some straw. Then he ran to the entrance to the building and went down the stairs into the cellar, where the barrel had been placed in its center, and a board provided to lean against the barrel. With a penknife, Hamilton pinned one end of the cloth to this board, then unrolled the cloth, onto which he then placed the straw, poured the oil of camphene and sprinkled a trail of gunpowder. While he was doing this, Cox said to Wenman, "Do you think this will work? Have we enough powder?"

"We had better," replied Wenman. "If this ain't enough, there's no powder left on this island. I hear the Marines are bringing some more in from Brooklyn, and from Governor's Island. But what with this high wind and deep freeze, it's any-body's guess whether they'll get here in time or not. You know what, Cox: if you've got an in with the Almighty, this might be a good time to start praying."

Hamilton had finished preparing the fuse. "It's ready, boys. And since I went to the trouble of preparing this fuse, shouldn't I have the honor of firing it?"

"Well, James," said Wenman, lighting a candle, "you shall."

He handed the lit candle to Hamilton, and then he and Cox ran out of the building, leaving Hamilton to light the fuse. Hamilton did so, then raced to join the other three outside the building, where a crowd had gathered. The four men got the crowd to back off, telling them there would be a big explosion. They waited...and nothing happened.

"What, did the fuse go out?" said Hamilton, who started back toward the building, only to hear someone shout, "It's going up the barrel, now!"

Again the crowd backed off, and this time a massive explosion not only brought down the entire front of the building, but also part of the adjacent building, which caught fire.

"Oh my God," cried the Mayor, "we're going to need more powder! I hope those Marines get here in time."

On the East River, the Fulton Street Ferry was attempting to cross from Brooklyn to Manhattan. On it was a detachment of Marines, led by Captain Mix of the U.S. Navy, together with Charles King, the Editor of the *New York American*, and future President of Columbia College. They had with them six barrels of gunpowder. As they headed toward Manhattan, they beheld something horrific—the lower part of Manhattan had become an inferno. The heat was so intense and the rain of fire so ruinous, that the tops of some of the masts on the docked ships were now ablaze. On Front Street, a saltpeter warehouse exploded, filling the air with screaming streams of multi-colored flashes. At the water's edge, barrels of turpentine ignited their own soul wracking terror, with the flaming liquid flowing into the East River, making it look as if the frozen water itself were on fire, along with everything else. Almost all the men stared open mouthed—apparently hypnotized by the appalling sight. But Captain Mix said, "Easy, men—don't lose your nerve. That beast out there is strong, but so what? You know what to do with fear: you're *Marines*—never forget it!

Flames

In Manhattan, amidst all the smoke and flame and mad fury of the moment, with men frantically trying to save their property, or steal the property of others, or use what small resources they had to fight the inferno, Captain Mix appeared leading his detachment of Marines, who carried with them six kegs of gunpowder. Charles King was with them. The detachment paused before a church on Wall Street near Broad Street. Captain Mix turned to King and said, "Is this the place we're supposed to meet the Mayor?"

"Yes, it is."

"Well, where is he?"

"I don't know; being the Mayor, he probably has his hands full."

"Well, in case you haven't noticed, King, we've got *our own* hands full—of gunpowder—six kegs of it! I'm not doing a damn thing without the Mayor's say-so. You get him here, quick!"

In Hanover square the Mayor himself was besieged by a crowd of people terrified by the towering flames, while King plunged into the crowd, trying to make his way to the Mayor—whose courage was proving crucial in this battle against the flames.

On Broad Street, led by the Mayor, the detachment of Marines was marching down the road carrying 4 kegs of powder. Captain Mix called a halt and ordered the men to remove their jackets and cover the kegs lest they ignite—it was raining fire. The men obeyed. As they set off again, their feet started to slip and slide on the ice. "Careful, men," called Captain

Mix, "don't fall with that stuff—else we'll all get to Hell a lot sooner than we planned."

"What do you mean, *get* to Hell," cried a Marine, "we're there now!"

As the men were approaching 52 Exchange Place, the cries were heard: "Clear the streets, the Marines are coming!" Then the Marines plunged into the cellar.

In the cellar of 52 Exchange Place, at 5 or 6 in the morning, the intrepid Captain Mix lit the slow fuse; his Marines ran madly up the stairs and into the street, while Mix, his hands in his pockets, strolled out nonchalantly, whistling a tune as if nothing were going to happen. A few moments after he appeared on the street, the entire building sank into the ground as if it were sinking into water. There was applause, and the Mayor pointed to the flames and announced, "This monster will not cross Broad Street, after all! If it wants to spread, it'll have to try some other direction than Northwest. We've blocked it, boys! When we do the same in a few other places, this beast is beaten!"

At the corner of Pine and William Streets, a weary Nehemias Cone, aided by his daughter Rachel, and by Ezekiel Bloom, otherwise known as Egmont Blühen, were carrying into his shop some of the merchandise they had removed earlier, when the threat of destruction seemed imminent. "I think that does it," said Nehemias. "Thanks to you," he said to Ezekiel, "we were able to save the merchandise, and we'll be able to sleep tonight with a roof over our heads, because of your putting out that burning ember overhead. I can't thank you enough."

Flames

"Rachel's safety and yours are the only thanks I need, sir. If it were in my power, I would prevent any misfortune from ever coming to either of you."

"I thank you with all my heart, Ezekiel—or should I call you Egmont?"

"Perhaps I should go into the kitchen and make some tea—would either of you like that?" Rachel said.

Both men signaled assent, and Rachel went into the kitchen.

"Tell me, young man," said Nehemias Cone, "what is your real name? When we first met, you let me think it was Ezekiel, but Rachel said you told her it was Egmont, and that you weren't even Jewish."

"I'm Jewish all right," Blühen said, "and I came over here when I was ten. I was all alone. My father's parting words to me were, *keep your Jewishness secret.* That was because my mother was murdered in the Hep Hep riots, and he was afraid for me."

"I'm terribly sorry to hear all this. It was for her, then, that you were saying Kaddish?"

"For her and for my father, who I learned passed away recently."

"Terrible."

"But now, I can live openly as Jew—and I want to."

"Hm. You say you came here when you were ten? That must mean you never were Bar Mitzvah."

"That's right."

"It's a good way for you to start—ascend the Bimah as a Bar Mitzvah."

"At my age? I'm twenty-five!"

"It's never too late," said Nehemias.

"It will be strange—I have no parents any more, nobody over here even to give me a Bar Mitzvah present."

"Aren't you forgetting me?" said Rachel, entering with the tea things. "I might give you a Bar Mitzvah present."

"Really? What might you give me?"

"Myself—that is, if Father consents, and you still want me."

"I consent—cheerfully," Nehemias said.

"And as for me," said Ezekiel, "I have never stopped wanting you."

"Baruch Hashem!" cried Nehemias. "First the fire—then this! Hashem works in mysterious ways."

Shortly afterwards in the second story of Thaddeus' Bender's house on 4th Street, Dr. DeLeo, his hands and apron smeared with blood, and his assistant, Beatrice, likewise blood spattered, were washing their hands. Sean's head was swathed in bandages. "His temple was slightly creased with the bullet," the doctor told Emily, "and he was knocked out. But I don't think there's any really serious damage; he should be all right." Emily embraced the startled physician, who said, "don't thank me; thank *the Lord*. Sean is a lucky man. Keep him quiet for at least three weeks—give him a chance to get his strength back."

All had departed from the patient's room except Emily and Benjamin. "Thank you so much, Benjamin," she said, "for everything. You covered yourself with glory."

"No, no," said Benjamin. "The hero is Sean, here. He saved your father's life—possibly yours as well."

Flames

"If you hadn't the courage to tangle with that crazy man, one of us might well have been killed. *You* might have been killed. You're both heroes to me."

Beatrice poked her head in the door, and she said, *sotto voce,* "Why don't you two speak in the hall? You'll wake him up."

"I'm not leaving his side," Emily said. She reached up to kiss Benjamin. "Thank you, dear Benjamin. We have to talk—but right now I'm too tired. We'll talk tomorrow—is that all right?"

"Whatever you want is fine with me, Emily," Benjamin said, "I see how things are."

"You're a wonderful man, Benjamin Livingston."

He made a slight bow to her, and left the room, closing the door quietly.

Emily knelt at the side of the unconscious Sean, who opened his eyes at that moment and, seeing her, looked at her with a worried expression. She kissed the furrow between his brows, then took his hand and kissed it, also. Sean smiled faintly, closed his eyes, and went back to sleep.

Flames

Twenty-Seven
Later that morning

Thaddeus was in his small study at home. He heard a faint knock on the door, and without his invitation, the door opened. Emily came in, and closed the door behind her. "How's the fireman?" Thaddeus asked.

"He's sound asleep. He woke up briefly last night, smiled at me, then closed his eyes and dropped off again. When I left him a moment ago, he hadn't moved a muscle or said a word in all that time."

"So you haven't been to bed yet."

"I can't sleep until I know he's going to be all right."

"It sounds like you still love him."

"I do. Very much."

"Does your fiancé know this?"

"He guesses it. But I'm telling him today."

"And breaking off the engagement?"

"How could I marry him? It wouldn't be honest."

"The time for honesty was when he proposed to you."

"I made a mistake, I admit it. But you are scarcely entitled to lecture me about honesty, Father."

At first, Thaddeus was at a loss for something to say. Then, he managed: "Emily, let me ask: did you *really* not know what my occupation has been? Everyone else seems to have known."

"I think...I didn't *want* to know. So I found ways to push the truth away. I thought to myself: I don't have to worry about this because Daddy has given me his word. When at last the truth came crashing in, I felt guilty—not only because of

213

how the money supporting me was earned, but also because, deep down, *I had known it all the time*—but was afraid to acknowledge the truth. Which is, Father, that you and I have been accomplices to the slave master. When Sean pointed it out, I was angry at him. I was unjust to him; I treated him badly. And I felt ashamed to show my face in public."

"You must hate me."

"No, Daddy, I love you."

"How can you? I lied to you."

"You sure did. And Daddy, I was furious! So angry, in fact, that if I let it control me, it might have killed me. So I kept telling myself that you did very well with the hand you were dealt, and that I might not have done nearly so well in the same circumstances."

"That's very kind—and maybe too generous."

"Maybe. But you showed yourself willing to take a bullet for me. There's no getting around that. And most everything else you've done has been for love of me—including giving me the chance to be a philanthropist. I love being charitable and generous. Thanks to you, it's a pleasure I hope to enjoy to the hilt."

"Well, just now you've been very charitable and generous to *me*, and I hope to find ways to thank you for it."

"How can you do that?"

"To start in a small way, by sharing with you my decision to diversify my business. What I currently do is not only morally questionable, it's also risky: I rely too much on the success of a single crop! All it would take would be some pest, some weevil or other, or something else unforeseen—a war, for God's sake—to destroy southern cotton, and I'd have a slew of bad debts on my books. It's bound to happen, sooner or later, and when it does, it could ruin us. So I'm going to do less of cotton and more of other things—Northern Real Estate, for instance."

"It's the right thing to do so far as it goes, but it's not nearly enough."

"I hear you," said Thaddeus.

"Good. May I ask you to thank me also in another way?"

"By supporting your marriage to Sean?"

"That's it exactly."

"Will he have you?"

"I hope so."

"Then he hasn't proposed yet?"

"Daddy, he's flat on his back—give him a chance!"

"I'll give him as much of a chance as you like. Still, it's good to have a plan to fall back on."

"That would be a nunnery for me, and a life of service to God. Those are *my* consequences."

Thaddeus gave his daughter a look of deep admiration. "I'm so proud of you," he said. "You're a grown up woman."

"That's what I hope to be—if not now, then soon."

"And if I want grandchildren," he ventured, "I'd best encourage your union with Sean, is that right?"

"You could do a lot worse. I'm sure that with Sean as the father, I'll have many beautiful children."

"Dearest Emily, I can't wait."

"Neither can I. I know what I want, and I'm going for it with everything in me."

"That's my girl! I felt the same way at your age." Thaddeus put loving hands on her shoulders, and beamed down at her. Then having made a decision, said: "I have some business downtown. Is it all right if I go, or would you prefer me to stay?"

"No Daddy, that's all right; you can go," she said. "And thank you for *everything.*"

"I understand," he said, "and I'll be leaving in a moment." Father and daughter exchanged a smile and an unspoken understanding.

At that moment, the front door bell rang. Emily raced downstairs to answer it, and opened the door to find Benjamin with Katherine. "Katherine wanted to come," Benjamin said, "I hope it's all right."

"Of course it is," Emily said. "I'm glad to see you, Katherine."

"How is our hero?" Katherine asked.

"When I left a few minutes ago, he was still sleeping. He woke up briefly last night, but he hasn't woken up since then. I'm a little worried."

Katherine went to Emily and embraced her. "Don't you worry, Emily," she said. "He's going to be just fine, with you tending him."

Emily started to feel tears welling up, so she cleared her throat and said, "had it not been for Benjamin, Sean might not be here to tend, or I might not be around to tend him."

"Oh God," said Katherine, "to lose two dear friends at once?! I can't bear the thought."

"You *are* a good friend," Emily said, and I can be no less." She turned to Benjamin. "Dear Benjamin," she said, "dear faithful, loving Benjamin, I beg you to release me from my vow to you—I should never have made it in the first place. Sean is the only one I can love with my entire self."

Flames

"I've always feared that," Benjamin said, "But I had hoped to be able to bring you closer to me."

"I should go into another room," Katherine said.

"No, no, sweet Katherine," said Emily, "this concerns you as well." Emily turned to Benjamin. "Give me your hand, my dear. I cannot provide you with the kind of passionate love you deserve, but the one who *can* is standing as close to you as Katherine, here." She joined Benjamin's hand to Katherine's. "I'm so grateful to you both, and the finest gift I can give you both is—each other."

"I don't know what to say," said Benjamin.

Beatrice appeared. "Sean is starting to stir," she said.

Emily spoke to Benjamin: "There's plenty for you to say, my dear, but not to me. Say it to Katherine; she's eager to hear it."

Emily ran up the stairs and into the bedroom where Sean was now sitting up. "My darling," she cried, "you're awake!

"Your darling, am I?"

"I hope no one else's."

"*I* have no one else, Emily."

"What about those two young women you were with not so long ago?"

"Not so long ago? That was *a year* ago!"

"I have a long memory."

"It was a church social. They were my cousins, for heaven's sake! I didn't want to go—certainly not with *them*—but my mother made me."

"A reasonable story, I suppose."

"It's the truth. But how'd you get yourself a fiancé? Did your father make you do that?"

"No—I have no one but myself to blame for that. But it's over. I just broke off the engagement, downstairs."

"I'm glad. You should never have made it in the first place."

"You're right. I was stupid."

"You accepted him because you were stupid?"

"Well...that, and...the fact that he asked me. A proposal can be very persuasive."

"So it's proposal time, is it?

"If you're not up to it, I can wait."

"Oh, I'm up to it, all right. But not like this. Dirty and smelly as I am, I'm not fit to propose to anyone—least of all to you. I need to bathe."

"But Dr. DeLeo said that for the first three weeks you should be as still as possible."

"What do these doctors know? If I don't clean up, I'm a health hazard for the whole city!"

Emily clapped her hands, and Beatrice appeared immediately. "Beatrice," Emily said, "could you prepare a bath for Mr. Dougherty?"

"Yes, Miss Emily. The hot water won't take long. I'll bring it up as soon as it's ready." And with that, Beatrice disappeared, leaving the two alone again.

"Is New York still burning, Emily?"

"Here and there. They had to blow up three or four buildings to stop the fire from spreading. But the worst is over."

"I wish I was there to help. That's my job."

"Your first job is to get better. Otherwise you'll be no use to anyone—including me."

Flames

"I gotta get a message to Mr. Tappan—so he knows I'm not faking anything. Not that it will matter if the warehouse has burned down."

"We've already sent word to him—and told him you'd be back to work as soon as the doctor says you're able."

"What about my mother?"

"We've also sent word to her as well—told her the doctor said not to worry."

"You've taken care of everything! And to think you braved the fire! Must have scared the b'jesus out of you."

"It did. At one point I nearly fainted dead away. But I willed myself to keep going; I had to find you."

"Amazing!"

"Not so amazing—I happen to love you."

There was a brief pause and then he said, "It's better I am at showing these things than saying 'em."

"Have you had many girl friends, Seanie?"

"There were a few that caught my eye, but none of that went anywhere. None of 'em was special enough, and besides, my Ma didn't like any of 'em. And she was right."

"Your mother doesn't like me either."

"It's the *idea* of you she doesn't like. She really doesn't know what an angel you are—how beautiful you are on the inside as well as outside. But when she sees how much I love you, she'll be won over."

"How much you love me? There, you said it! That wasn't so hard, was it?"

"The words just came out. But I hope that in a little while I'll be able to show it so strong you'll feel...the whole might of me behind it."

"It sounds...wonderful...!"

Meanwhile, Benjamin and Katherine were heading back to Bloomingdale in the Livingstons' carriage. Although there was plenty of room for them to sit next to each other, they sat facing each other on opposite benches.

"So now that you cannot have your first choice," Katherine was saying, "you want to fall back on me—second best, apparently. How do you think that makes me feel?"

For a few moments, only the sound of the carriage wheels and the horses' hooves filled the carriage. When Benjamin finally did speak, it seemed as if all his customary ebullience had drained out of him: "I have no words," he finally managed, "except to say I've been a fool...a fool to think I had to leave home to find happiness...and a fool to think I could find it with someone who never really wanted me in the first place...while all the time my joy was waiting for me here...right here at home, *with you*...but I was too blind to see it. I beg you to forgive me. If you cannot, I won't blame you, for I cannot forgive myself for all the pain I've caused you." Benjamin covered his face with his hands, and bent forward, as if the weight of his own folly was too much for him.

Katherine leaned forward, and placed her hand on his head. "I do forgive you, Benjy, because I've loved you forever, and I'm not going to stop now."

Benjamin knelt in front of her, and took her hands in his. "You'll never be sorry," he said.

She smiled down at him. "Is that a promise?"

"I dedicate my life to it," he said.

Meanwhile, in the sick-room at Thaddeus Bender's Fourth Street home, Beatrice entered with clean sheets, towels, a wash cloth, soap, and a bucket of steaming hot water. She poured the hot water into a small metal bathing tub, which provided a metal shelf on which the bather could sit while giving him or herself a sponge bath. "There it is, folks," said Beatrice. "The water's a little hot right now, but in a few minutes it'll be just right. Let me know if you need anything." And Beatrice left them.

Sean began to rise from the bed, but then stopped short. "If it wouldn't be troubling you too much, Emily, I'd rather you left the room while I bathed."

"You're in my house now," she said, "and the house rules are that when the husband bathes, the wife can remain in the room if she likes—in fact the wife can *help* if she likes."

"So we're husband and wife?" he said.

"We will be, very soon, otherwise you can leave the house now—without breakfast!"

"And without clothes, too?"

"No, no. You'll get your clothes back. After we stripped you last night, I had Beatrice wash *all* your clothes—they needed it! They should be dry by now."

"I want my breakfast."

"You can have it—if you pay the price."

"Which is..."

"Marriage to me. Are you ready for it?"

"Very. One of the reasons I wanted you to leave is so you wouldn't see just how ready I am."

"I already can tell *that*. What I mean is, are you ready to say it out loud, in the church, before the whole congregation?"

"I'm ready. I swear it on the souls of our children."

"But we don't have any."

Paul R. Cooper

"A lack which we will soon fix—if I have anything to say about it."

"I'll give you *everything* to say about it."

And with that, she proceeded to bathe him, lovingly. As she passed the washcloth over his back and broad shoulders, she said, "My friends always told me that my father had a mountain of money. But I never felt rich until this moment."

"But the money doesn't hurt."

"In a way it does," she said as she soaped up his arm.

"You mean, considering where it comes from—slavery and all?"

"Exactly. How can we rail against these ill-gotten gains, when we ourselves benefit from them?" By this time, she was lovingly passing the washcloth over his chest.

He tried to speak. "Well, do you propose to...to...I can't think while you're doing that."

What she was doing was tenderly laving his nipples.

"I'm sorry," she said. "I'll stop till you can get the thought out."

"What I wanted to ask," he said, "is this: do you propose to rely only on my small income? It's pretty Spartan even for just one person, let alone a family. You may want to think of some compromise between our principles and the family's comfort."

"Well, here's what I've been thinking: we wouldn't give away *all* our income," she said, resuming the laving. "I think we should keep what we need for our modest requirements, and use the rest to help others. How does that sound?" But before he could answer, she was looking down at the treasures below. "Oo-oo-oo, that is *amazing!* May I wash down there?"

"Go ahead—just be careful."

"Oh, I'll be so careful..." And, with exquisite care, she proceeded to wash the parts that she had lately speculated about, but was now seeing for the first time.

"Ohhh, it all feels so good..." he sighed.

"What I'm doing?"

"Yes of course, but also...also..."

Sensing his difficulty, she said, "A new thought? I'll stop till you can get that one out, too."

"I was trying to say that it's not only what you're doing, but also what you're *saying* that feels so right. I have to tell you, Emily: you're more than an angel. You're the woman I've always wanted."

They kissed.

"Darling," she said, continuing the washing, "we're going to be beautiful together. I love you so much."

At length, he rose from the bath, and she patted him dry. "Now I feel clean!" he said.

"Are you ready for breakfast?"

He gazed at her with frank ardor. "I'm very hungry."

They heard a knock on the door, causing Sean to dive underneath the covers. It was Beatrice, who entered and told them that Arthur Tappan had come to pay Sean a visit, if he was up to it.

"Oh my God!" said Emily, "do we show him upstairs?"

"He's *already* up," said Beatrice, "he's just waiting for your consent before coming in."

"Show him in," said Sean; "he's made an effort to come here, and we should respect that."

Beatrice opened the bedroom door, and Arthur Tappan came in. "Dear lad!" he said, "We've heard all about it. Thanks be to God you're safe. And look what a lovely young nurse you have attending you!"

"Mr. Tappan," said Arthur, "this is Emily Bender. You met her a year ago at the Chatham Street Chapel."

"Ah yes?"

"Finney was preaching."

Tappan doffed his hat and bowed. "I think I remember. A pleasure to meet you again, my dear. Do take care of young Sean; he's very important to us."

"I'll do my best," said Emily.

"And as for you, Sean, please don't worry about work. Although it's true that the warehouse has burned down, I've already given orders to rebuild it, and I'll need all the good men I can get. So when you're ready for work, your job will be waiting for you, with more work to do than ever." He turned to Emily. "Is there anything at all you need, Miss Bender, anything I can provide?"

"No thank you, Mr. Tappan," Emily murmured, "your coming to see Sean has been a big boost to him, and to all of us."

"In that case, I will take my leave. Goodbye to you both, and God bless you!"

"Thank you sir," chorused Sean and Emily.

After giving Emily a covert wink, Beatrice showed Arthur Tappan out of the bedroom. After he had gone, Sean exclaimed, "Can you beat that? They say that man makes a million dollars a year, and yet he has time to visit a lowly employee."

"He must be a saint," said Emily.

"Well, yes and no. If you make a mistake at work, he can come down on you so hard that you wish the ground would open up and swallow you. But let anything happen to you, he becomes an angel of mercy. He's hard to figure out—but I like him a lot. He's a good man, is Arthur Tappan."

"He sure is."

"And now where were we, when we were interrupted? As if I could forget it."

Helpfully, Emily offered: "I think you were talking about how hungry you were?"

"I still am—hungrier than ever. But..."

"But...?"

"I have a confession to make..."

"A confession...?"

"I'm embarrassed about it..."

"Whatever it is...don't be embarrassed. It's all right. You can tell me."

"Well...the truth is...this is my first time."

"Oh, darling!"

"I put on a big act in the firehouse...like I'm the manliest hero of romance. Because, in the firehouse, you have to...they expect it. In there, they think the more experience a man has, the better it will be for his bride on the wedding night. Because *somebody* has to know what they're doing, right? So they all go around trumpeting their latest exploits, and I boast about all kinds of fake stuff just to keep pace with them. But the truth is...well, you know what the truth is. I'm sorry."

"Oh darling, until you said that, I had no idea of how much I could love a man. You're a beginner like me? How beautiful! We'll find our way together. Whatever you do, it will be wonderful, because it will be you doing it, and be-

225

cause...you'll be giving me...what nobody else has received. I want you more than I can say."

Once again they heard knocking on the door, and once again Sean dove into the bed.

"Come in," Emily called, half croaking the words.

Beatrice poked her head in the door. "Sean's mother has arrived."

"Heavens!" Emily exclaimed. "I better help her up the stairs."

"No need for *that*, Miss Bender," said Megan Dougherty as she walked in, her cane tapping an angry tattoo on the floor boards. "I may be old, but I'm not decrepit." She saw her son in the bed. "Saints preserve us, did they try to kill you, darlin' boy?"

"Yes, someone did try," Sean said, "but his aim was bad, and I was only grazed."

"You've been keeping the wrong company, Seanie, that's what you've been doing."

"You stop it right there, Ma. As soon as this bandage comes off, Emily and I are getting married. And if you want us married Catholic, then you keep a civil tongue in your head, do you understand? It's no longer funny. Now what have you to say to Emily, here?"

Megan cast a disbelieving look at her son. "I'm goin' to send word to your Da: that wound has addled your brains, Sonny. Otherwise you'd never dare talk to your old Mother this way."

"I may be weak, but I've never felt saner in my life. Now you turn and face Emily, and say to her what's long over-due, otherwise—if God should bless us with children—you'll be lucky to be invited to the baptism."

Flames

Emily found her voice. "You're being too harsh, Seanie. She's your mother, after all. I don't want our marriage to start under a cloud. Please be nicer to her."

"If anybody else had said that to me," Sean said, "I would have shrugged it off. But since it's you, Emily...I'll try to be nicer to Ma—but she has to apologize to you first. Go ahead, Ma."

There was a pause while Megan grasped the situation. Then she turned to Emily, and said, very quietly, "Emily, I am indeed sorry for how I've treated you. I'm no longer in Ireland; I must try to remember that. I must get used to the new ways. And the truth is, Seanie's found a good woman in you, and you deserve better from me, and I'll try to *do* better. I apologize."

"Oh, Mrs. Dougherty, please don't upset yourself further about this. I love your son with everything in me, and I'll try to be a good wife to him. But I have a favor: would you allow me to call you 'Mother'? My own mother died when I was born, and it would be a comfort to me if you could be—every now and again—a mother to me. I'd like that."

"Oh, and I'd love it, too, darlin' Emily," said Megan, embracing her. And if, from time to time, I seem to be behaving *too much* like the Irish Mammy, then do be slipping a quiet word in my ear. I may be getting old, but I can still hear every little thing. And now, I think I better be getting home, lest I be overstaying my welcome."

Emily and Sean protested otherwise, but Megan said she knew better. She opened the door, turned and blew them a kiss, then closed it. Emily and Sean heard her voice through the closed door: "Thank you very much, Miss Beatrice, but I can find my own way downstairs and out. I'm not *that* old."

Then they heard the heavy clumping of her cane-aided foot-falls on the stairs.

Beatrice opened the door and stuck her head in the doorway. "Anything more I can do for you, children?"

"No thank you, Beatrice," said Emily, "except what we'd really like is for visiting time to be over."

"Don't worry, child, I'll stand guard."

Emily brought a towel to Sean.

"What's that for? I'm dry already."

"It's to keep you from catching cold while I'm making the bed with fresh sheets."

Which she did. After she finished, she covered Sean with the fresh sheets and blankets. Said Emily: "Now don't go anywhere!"

"You don't have to worry," Sean said.

Emily went to snuff out the oil lamp, but Sean said, "oh, please! Leave it up, if you don't mind. I want to see you."

"I'm a little shy...but I will if it's important..."

"It is to me...but...you gotta feel right about it. So you can snuff out the light, if you want to."

"Thank you, darling." She continued to the lamp and was about to extinguish it, when she stopped. "No...we'll leave it burning bright, if it pleases you..."

She slowly disrobed; Sean's eyes filled with the sight of her. When the bright flame of her body was fully revealed, she said, "Am I all right? Are you pleased with me?"

"You're beautiful," he said, "I don't know how I got to be so lucky."

Now they were under the covers. Sean said, "Do you really think we should be doing this—your father being here and all?"

Flames

"He's left the house. I got the feeling that he knew we might prefer it, so he left us alone for our sake. It means that the only reason not to do this is if either of us doesn't feel like it."

"Well I sure feel like it," Sean said.

"I'm glad," said Emily, because I do, too—very much."

Sean placed his hand on Emily's thigh, then removed it almost immediately, as if it scalded him. "What's the matter, darling?" she asked.

"I never knew how rough and coarse my hands are," he said, "until they touched your skin. It's so silky smooth, I'm afraid I might scratch it."

"If you did, then I'd welcome it. I love your touch, Seanie, and I love the strength of you."

Very gently, tentatively, he placed his hand on her breast. She covered his hand with her own, and pressed it into her flesh. "Don't worry," she said, "I'm no Dresden china doll; you can use me."

"I will," he said, and proceeded to put her lovingly and passionately to the use he had imagined for so long in all his secret dreams.

"Darling," she whispered, "you're wonder—" But her word was cut off by his mouth covering hers. Her fingers, splayed on his back, felt the rippling power of him. Soon she sensed that the moment had come for her to help him, and she reached down to position him. "This way, darling..."

But he saw her wince, and he hesitated..."I'm hurting you."

"It's what I want," she whispered. "Please...go ahead...burn me up."

His climax came not long after, and though she did not climax, her face shone with a supernal happiness: she knew she had received the gift that nobody else had ever received, or ever would receive.

"Now can I feed you supper?" she asked. "What would you like?"

"More of the same," he murmured.

"Really! Are all firemen like you?"

But he was asleep on her breast.

Flames

Twenty-Eight
Six weeks later

In the majestic interior of New York's St Patrick's Cathedral, there was a wedding going on—between Emily and Sean. After the ceremony, in the reception area, they greeted their friends and family. Among the first to be greeted were Katherine and Benjamin.

"You beat us to the altar, Ben!" cried Sean. "How's marriage treating you?"

"I'm the luckiest person in the world," said Benjamin. "Katherine loves me, and I can't imagine a glory greater than that."

"Overhearing them, Martha Livingston popped up out of nowhere and said, "Didn't I tell you? Didn't I keep saying that Katherine was the one for you? Didn't I tell you? Wasn't I right?"

"As I keep telling *you*, mother, you were right, right, right, and I was wrong, wrong, wrong. Which proves again that I'm lucky—even in my mother."

"Listen to him!" cried Martha.

"Not when he says he's luckier in love," said Katherine, "don't listen to him then. He's not the lucky one—I am."

"Seanie and never have that fight," said Emily, "as to who's the luckier. When I say I'm the luckier, Sean, sweetheart that he is, doesn't want to contradict me!"

Megan Dougherty appeared, accompanied by a heavyset man who looked to be Sean's father.

"Da!" cried Sean, and the two embraced. "I'm so glad you could make it!" said Sean, genuinely pleased.

"Wouldn't miss it," replied the elder Dougherty. "Looks like you got yourself a peach, Sonny."

"Thank you, Mr. Dougherty," said Emily sweetly, curtseying.

"The name's Glendon," he said, "but if you like, you can call me Da—or whatever you want. For now that I think of it, seeing you two together, I believe Boston's too far away for me to be working."

Megan laughed, then said, "It took him only five years to figure that out—which for my husband here is quicker thinking than usual. And as for you, Seanie boy, don't you go telling Emily that she's luckier than you. That's plumb wrong. To have found a queen like her makes *you* the lucky one, and don't you forget it."

"Thanks, Mother," Emily said, "Your good words mean a lot to me."

Edward Bass and his wife Sarah appeared, a babe in her arms.

"Oo-oo-oo, how cute!" Emily cooed. "He's so beautiful!"

"Naturally," said Edward. "Takes after my side of the family."

"Really, my love?" said his wife, "I thought he takes more after *my* side."

"Well, Sarah, I'm just telling you what I think."

"Of course, dear," said Mrs. Bass, "I'll try to pay more attention." Then Sarah Bass turned to the bridal couple and said with a smile, "normally, if Edward says it's so, then it *must* be so. He knows almost everything."

Arthur Tappan came to greet them. "Ah! You married your nurse. A shrewd choice! You both showed good judgment."

Flames

"And *you* showed good judgment in hiring Sean!" said Emily.

"You are correct, Mrs. Dougherty—but apparently you are in the habit of being correct."

"Not all the time," said Emily. "But this time I was lucky enough to learn the error of my ways before it was too late."

A liveried serving lady approached with a tray of hors d'oeuvres. "Perhaps the bride would fancy one of these," she said, "I made them myself."

Emily did a double take: "Mrs. Gallagher! How wonderful to see you! But how...?"

"Miss Beatrice told your father I could use the work, and...here I am!"

"I'm so glad! But who is taking care of the children?"

"Oh—Bessie is."

"Bessie?"

"Bessie Simon," said Mrs. Gallagher, "you know, Joe Simon's widow?"

"Of course I know—but that's wonderful!" Emily exclaimed. "Then you two are..."

"We're friends, Mrs. Dougherty...more than friends, actually. Whenever Bessie takes in a big load of sewing or washing, she drops off her children at my house, or I take mine to hers so I can help with the work. And if I can get an occasional job as a cook or maid, Bessie helps me out—just like today. She really is a very fine woman."

"You *both* are," said Emily, reaching for an hors d'oeuvre. After eating it, she said, "this is delicious, Mrs. Gallagher. But the news you bring is even more so."

In another part of the reception area, Mayor Lawrence was greeting Thaddeus Bender: "Congratulations, Thaddeus; they make a handsome couple. Are you pleased?"

"Couldn't be happier."

"Glad to hear it. It's a very advantageous marriage from the groom's point of view."

"It's a very advantageous marriage from *my* point of view, Cornelius. He's a good lad, and a promising one—very bright. I can use him! But we're not talking business, here."

"Too bad: Let's *talk* business. What are the prospects for the market?"

"Not good, I'm afraid. What with all this giddy land speculation, this banking uncertainty, with too much paper being issued, the fundamentals are unsound. I wouldn't be surprised if there's a panic in a few months. And if there is, the devastation it causes will make the Great Fire look like child's play."

"That's what I think, too. Looks like I'd better start hedging my bets."

"That's what *I'm* doing."

At that moment, Ezekiel and Rachel appeared.

"Egmont!" cried Thaddeus, "wonderful to see you—and with Rachel Cone on your arm?"

"She's my fiancée," Ezekiel said. "And my name isn't really Egmont; it's Ezekiel."

"Truly? That means you're converting?"

"No, Mr. Bender, I'm already Jewish—have been since I was born. I just didn't tell anyone. I thought you'd want to be one of the first to know."

"Indeed! This may put a new complexion on things. This is worth thinking about."

Flames

Mayor Lawrence spoke up: "Before you think too hard, Thaddeus, isn't this the young man you described as being your right arm—on whom you could rely to do the most challenging assignments?"

"Indeed it is. Mayor Lawrence, may I present Ezekiel…" He turned to Ezekiel. "What's your last name changed to?"

"Bloom—it hasn't changed; it always *was* Bloom."

"Well then, Mr. Mayor, this is Ezekiel Bloom, who has done fine work for me."

"A pleasure to meet you Mr. Bloom," said the Mayor, who then turned to his friend. "Just think, Thaddeus, one of your star employees is getting married! His additional responsibilities deserve a raise in salary, don't you think?"

To Thaddeus Bender's credit, it took him little more than a moment to reply, "of course, that's not inappropriate."

"And I know," continued the Mayor, "that in addition, you'll want to celebrate the forthcoming nuptials by granting young Mr. Bloom a handsome bonus, isn't that right? Someone who could stage so lavish a wedding as this would certainly not want to forget the young man whose detective work helped make it possible—isn't *that* right?"

"I've met my match in you, Cornelius—but we always knew that!" said Thaddeus, who then turned to the engaged couple: "Ezekiel and Rachel," he said, "you will receive everything the Mayor suggests—and more—with my blessings."

"We thank both of you kind gentlemen," Rachel said, curtseying deeply.

Meanwhile, Emily and Sean had finally reached Beatrice.

"I owe you a lot, Miss Beatrice," said Sean. "If it hadn't been for you, Emily and I would never have found each other."

"Poor Beatrice," said Emily, "what will you do to keep yourself busy now that I am safely married?"

"You may be safely married, honey chile, but I understand that you and Sean are going to live with us for a while. And that will give me plenty to do—especially if God grants you a family. Which means, Mr. and Mrs. Dougherty, that if you haven't been practicing for a family before today, I suggest you get to it as soon as possible."

"Do not worry about a thing, Miss Beatrice," said Sean. "That thought has not escaped us."

END

21680601R00132

Made in the USA
Charleston, SC
26 August 2013